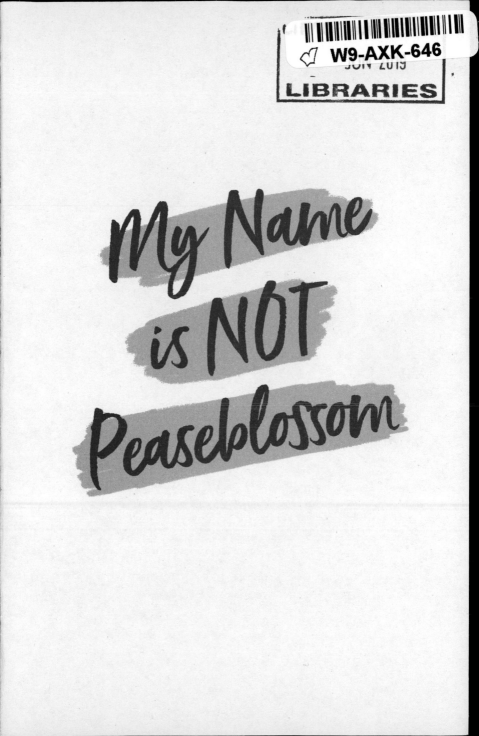

My Name is NOT Peaseblossom

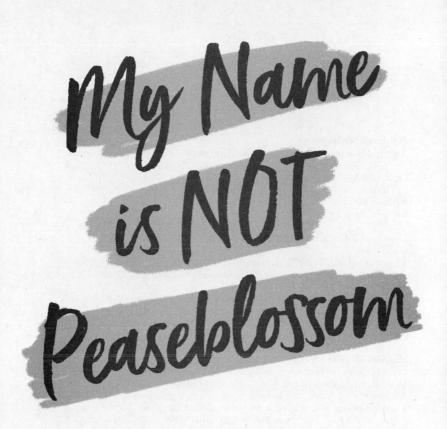

JACKIE FRENCH

📕 Angus&Robertson
An imprint of HarperCollins*Publishers*

Angus&Robertson

An imprint of HarperCollins*Publishers*, Australia

First published in Australia in 2019
by HarperCollins*Publishers* Australia Pty Limited
ABN 36 009 913 517
harpercollins.com.au

HarperCollins*Publishers*

Level 13, 201 Elizabeth Street, Sydney NSW 2000, Australia
Unit D1, 63 Apollo Drive, Rosedale, Auckland 0632, New Zealand
A 53, Sector 57, Noida, UP, India
1 London Bridge Street, London SE1 9GF, United Kingdom
2 Bloor Street East, 20th floor, Toronto, Ontario M4W 1A8, Canada
195 Broadway, New York NY 10007, USA

A catalogue record for this book is available
from the National Library of Australia

ISBN 978 1 4607 5478 8 (paperback)
ISBN 978 1 4607 0917 7 (ebook)

Cover design by Amy Daoud, HarperCollins Design Studio
Cover images by shutterstock.com
Author photograph by Kelly Sturgiss
Typeset in Sabon LT Std by Kirby Jones
Printed and bound in Australia by McPherson's Printing Group
The papers used by HarperCollins in the manufacture of this book are a
natural, recyclable product made from wood grown in sustainable plantation
forests. The fibre source and manufacturing processes meet recognised
international environmental standards, and carry certification.

To Mr Wm. Shakespeare,
the first begetter of these stories.
And to those who love,
everywhere and when.

CHAPTER 1

The early morning sun crouched on the dusty horizon.
I could feel its warmth on my wings as Puck and I flew
over the Amazons' camp. It smelled of horse-milk
cheese, leather tents and the adrenaline of the battle to
come.

Below us, the warrior women strapped on their leather
armour or checked the curved blades of their war axes.
Legend said Amazons' axes were forged from an iron
star that fell from the sky, and nothing could break a
star-forged axe. But no one who'd fought an Amazon
had lived to give the details.

All the warriors, even their horses, were gaunt.
Drought had eaten their land, and if they couldn't win
the right to graze these grasslands, they would all die of

starvation. Their children would die too, and their male slaves — for even Amazons needed men to breed with.

The children sat quiet and white-faced with their grandmothers, watching their mothers prepare for war. These girls knew what was happening today — and what would happen if the Amazons lost. Winning armies were never kind, not even to small girls and grandmothers.

'Hold on a moment, boy. I've got a cramp in my wing,' Puck called to me.

He perched on one of the leather tents, right above two Amazon warriors tightening their breast guards. I was glad Puck and I were no bigger than bees today. These women looked like they didn't take any nonsense.

I flew down next to him, fanning my wings to cool us off. Even so early in the day, heat shimmers rose from the grasslands around us.

'I don't see why we couldn't have TAPed right into the battle,' I complained.

TAP (time and place manipulation) was one of the best things about being a fairy — plus flying, magic potions and being almost immortal, as long as you didn't annoy their fairy majesties. Fairies who irritated King Oberon or Queen Titania tended to end up as mice or snails —

creatures that live short lives. Especially if Queen Titania commanded an attendant to stomp on them.

Puck winked at me. 'Listen, boy, if there's one thing I've learned in the past ten thousand years, it's to stop and admire the view.'

Ten thousand years of making potions! No wonder the old boy needed me along on a job like this. I glanced enviously at the blue buckskin breeches that Puck wore. He worked directly for King Oberon. Oberon's courtiers were allowed to wear silk hose and leather doublets too. The male attendants who worked for Queen Titania, like me, wore white rose-petal kilts, which were breezy in the nether regions, but she liked us to keep our chests bare.

But today I was doing something much more interesting than brushing Her Majesty's hair, or massaging her feet, or polishing dew drops. I'd been Puck's part-time apprentice for almost fifty years now, ever since the old boy's arthritis got too bad for him to crush snail shells fine enough. This was my first official role. And it was a big one. The flask of love potion in my belt was going to create one of the greatest romances of history, or my name wasn't Peaseblossom. That triumph would get me the job of Puck's permanent assistant, and his job when he retired. I'd never have to wear a rose petal again.

Every Midsummer's Eve, Queen Titania demanded two weddings must take place at her Midsummer Feast: first, a marriage of famous mortals to watch and laugh at before the revels began; and then a fairy wedding before the feast. This year the whole Fairy Court would watch me get married. But first we had to set up the mortals' wedding. Not easy, when the chosen bride and groom were going to try to kill each other today. But I had the potion and a plan.

I looked around the Amazons' camp, then at the fortress of Athens about five kilometres away, perched on its great rock.

'Come on,' I said to Puck, fluttering my wings impatiently. 'The Athenian army is coming out the gates.'

King Theseus led the way on his own small shaggy pony. Today he wore a helmet with blue feathers instead of a crown, but there was no doubt he was a king. He was already a legend among warriors — killer of the Minotaur.

His men followed him in their sweaty leather armour, their dark hair held back by leather bands, marching in formation across the grasslands towards us. Each soldier held his spears, with a dagger at his belt. The sun cracked into shards off their bronze shields and swords. Some rode shaggy horses, so small each rider's feet almost dragged on the ground.

Someone yelled a warning in the Amazon camp.

Queen Hippolyta strode forward to speak to her warriors as they lined up ready to face the Athenians: archers first, the long-legged horses of the cavalry behind. Hippolyta was almost two metres tall. Her trousers were stained with old blood, and her long blonde hair was tucked up under her leather helmet. She didn't look eager for battle. Great leaders never do.

She raised her voice and spoke calmly to each woman in her army. 'This battle is for the lives of our family and friends. Let all who fight today return to camp with their shield or on it! No coward's blood shall ever shame the name of the Amazon. Today we fight and live!'

Her army surged forward.

I looked at Puck.

He shrugged. 'Enjoy the sunlight, boy. It'll take them at least an hour to get into position. Armies don't move fast. They keep their energy for the battle.'

He took a flask from his belt and gulped a swig of what he claimed was arthritis potion. It smelled more like Dew Brew than essence of hedgehog.

Dust melded with sunlight as the many horses' hooves tore up the grass. At last both armies stopped about half a kilometre from each other, waiting for the word to charge. Above them an eagle soared, waiting. It knew it would feast on the dead tonight.

The King of Athens stepped forward, alone, sword in one hand, shield in the other. He marched with even steps towards the Amazon army. One of his men called to him, but Theseus didn't look back.

Queen Hippolyta gazed at him as he approached. She understood what he intended.

Puck and I knew too: it was standard for battles during this time. Theseus would offer terms for the Amazons' surrender. If Hippolyta accepted, no one need die today. Her people would live — until they starved. She would offer terms too. But no one — including Hippolyta — would expect Theseus to accept them.

'Come on!' I said, and made a beeline for the armies. Puck flapped slowly behind me.

Hippolyta said something to her nearest warrior, but I was still too far away to hear. She lifted the gold diadem from her head and gave it to the warrior to hold; then she hefted her shield and her war axe. By now I was hovering above her, still bee-sized, and heard her next words.

'If the Athenians attack while I negotiate with the King, behead each man. But spare the women in the city, and any boy child under the age of twelve.'

Hippolyta stepped towards King Theseus. I followed, a few metres above her. I had never heard such silence, despite the spears and axes held at the ready. No one seemed to breathe as Theseus and Hippolyta stopped about ten paces from each other.

Hippolyta spoke first. 'Surrender. If you lay down your arms, we will give you and your army three days to leave the city. We will spare any woman who chooses to remain here with her children.'

Theseus met her eyes. 'Men have held the rock of Athens since the first giants hurled it from the sky. There will be no surrender.'

'Our force is larger than yours, my women's weapons stronger.' Hippolyta's voice was almost gentle. She didn't want to kill these soldiers, nor the boys who would grow up to be Greek soldiers too, although she would if she had to. 'Our star iron can cut through bronze.'

'Not if the swordsman is quick enough.'

She smiled at that. 'Are you quick enough?'

Theseus didn't smile. 'Perhaps. The fortress on this rock has never fallen in man's memory. If you defeat us on this plain, we will draw back behind its walls. My people have food for a ten-year siege, and springs for water. Can your army sit here for ten years?'

'If we must. At least there is grass here.' Hippolyta looked at him seriously. 'While you hide behind the walls of your great fortress, we will harvest your wheat fields, your olive trees. There is no turning back for us. Our land is parched. The full moon led us here to what must be our new home.' She shrugged. 'There is nowhere further for us to go now, except into the sea.'

Theseus nodded. He too didn't seem to want this battle, but was ready to fight it. Theseus of Athens would never surrender. This was the man who had beaten a giant single-handedly at the isthmus and killed the Minotaur of Crete. He had never lost a battle.

'We will not retreat behind the fortress's walls,' he said shortly. 'We will not surrender. Our feet are on our native soil. Our blood will feed it as we die. It seems the blood of your people will also enrich our grass now.'

'Come on!' puffed Puck, catching up with me, wings flapping furiously. 'Use the potion.'

'Not yet,' I whispered. 'Something is happening.'

'Of course something is happening. Two armies are about to chop each other into pieces. Move, boy!'

'Not yet,' I said again.

Hippolyta nodded, as if she had expected Theseus's answer. 'There is a way only one person need die today,' she said quietly.

Theseus's eyebrows lifted. 'How?'

'We fight in single combat, you and I. If you lose, your army will open the city gates to us. Athens will be ours. If I lose, my army will depart.'

He frowned. 'Your women will follow your orders even when you are dead?'

'Of course. I have already told them what I planned. Will your men follow your orders?'

Again, Theseus assessed her. Was this a trick, he seemed to be wondering. Did she plan to kill him and then attack his leaderless army?

Slowly, he nodded. 'Wait here.'

'You were right,' said Puck, reluctantly admiring. 'I underestimated you, Peaseblossom. This is interesting.'

Most people did underestimate me. But if this went well, the Fairy Court would be talking about me for years.

'She's a true queen, just like he's a king,' I said. 'Both of them would sacrifice themselves for their people.'

Hippolyta stood calmly as Theseus walked back to his men. She held her axe lightly, gazing at the sky, the eagle and the sea beyond. This might be the last time she saw them. She was living each second that remained to her.

Puck and I waited too, our wings outstretched, balancing on the breeze. Probably no one would have noticed us even if we'd decided to be human-sized. All eyes were on the King. He spoke with several men, who must be his generals. Whispers rose from them, like wasps buzzing. A few called out in protest. Theseus hushed them with a lifted hand. Once more the Athenian army stood in silence beneath the sun.

Theseus walked back to meet the Queen. 'I agree to the terms,' he said. 'If I die, my army and my people will abandon the fortress and these lands. If you die, your army will depart.'

Of course his men had agreed, I thought. None of those Athenians could imagine a woman beating a hero like Theseus. But I had seen Amazons fight before. I suspected Theseus also knew how well they could fight. Would the Athenians follow their king's order and surrender if Theseus's blood spilled on the plain of Athens today? I doubted it. They would assume he had died by trickery, that no woman could slay a man in equal combat. And the Amazons — how would they react if their queen was killed?

Even as I thought it, Theseus asked again, 'Will your women really retreat as you have promised?'

'We keep our word,' Hippolyta said calmly. 'But I will not die today.'

Theseus did smile at that. 'Really? We will see.' He twirled …

Hippolyta hadn't expected the attack to be so swift, and yet she parried it, thrusting her shield up to meet his sword, leaving her axe arm free.

Puck nudged me, his wings shivering. His wings always quivered when he was excited. 'Get moving, Peaseblossom,' he hissed.

'I want to see who wins.'

'Who wins? If either of them wins, the other will be dead!'

'Who might win then. I don't think it's going to be a swift fight,' I added. 'Don't worry — I can slice a second into shreds. If one of them looks like landing a killing blow, I'll get there first.'

I gazed at the two warriors slashing and clashing on the battlefield. Theseus and Hippolyta knew each other's abilities now. You could almost feel them assess each other between each stroke.

Neither of their armies yelled encouragements or insults. They would not distract their champion in this critical combat.

'He's stronger and broader-shouldered, but she's taller and has a longer reach,' I said. 'I'd say they're equally matched.'

'I'd say that Her Majesty Queen Titania will turn you into a toad for the next two centuries if you mess up her midsummer fun,' Puck countered. His wings had turned pale pink with worry. 'Her Majesty won't want a royal bride with her nose cut off, or a groom who's lost his fingers. Do you want to be my permanent assistant or not, boy?'

'Of course I do!' I wanted this job so badly I could taste it. A job with true power …

'Then get in there with the heartsease juice, boy. Now! Hippolyta nearly had Theseus's arm off that time. You know Her Majesty demands perfection!'

'Don't get your wings in a twist. I'm going!'

I flew down, taking the long way through the army of Amazons. The women stood motionless as they watched their queen fight, their breasts and hard sweaty muscles bound tightly by their leather armour. I moved at the speed of light, but in fairy terms it was slow enough to see the colour of the warriors' eyes. Blue, mostly. Had there ever been an army as beautiful before or since?

Though their beauty was nothing to me, I reminded myself, as I swooped towards the King and Queen so fast it seemed his sword and her axe hung in the air. I was getting married in three days. My fiancée was the Fairy Floss, though everyone called her Flossie. I'd only met her once. She was First Assistant Tooth Fairy for the entire north-west region and had a fine career ahead of her. She was even pretty in a toothy kind of way, though it didn't matter if she hadn't been. A sprinkle of heartsease potion in our eyes at the wedding ceremony and Flossie and I would love each other forever.

Just like Theseus and Hippolyta would adore each other as soon as I managed to get the heartsease potion into their eyes.

I reached Theseus just as he kneeled to try to hack off Hippolyta's left leg. I squeezed the juice into his eyes, then flew up to her, hovering above her face as she brought her battle axe down towards his skull. I wondered briefly who she might have loved if I left her untouched by the potion. Assuming she lived, of course.

And was there a woman watching Theseus from the fortress walls? A woman he had loved last night and as he'd parted from her this morning? If there was, today would be as hard for her as if he'd died, for Theseus would never look at her again.

But my meddling was a good thing, I reminded myself. I wasn't just ensuring a grand royal wedding to begin Queen Titania's midsummer festivities — I was ending the war between two armies. Many people would have died here, if not for me. Instead, they would dance. And maybe Theseus and Hippolyta would have loved each other if they'd had the chance. Both were warriors, rulers. Both were willing to give their lives for their people. But we'd never know. A squirt of potion in each of their eyes and I'd changed their lives, and changed history too.

I fluttered back up to Puck, still bee-sized, grinning. I'd also made sure Her Majesty would have a fascinating Midsummer's Eve.

Hippolyta blinked, as if the world had been sepia and had suddenly gained colour. She lowered her axe. Her warriors murmured to each other.

Theseus had already flung his sword away. He looked at his hands: a soldier's hands, a king's hands and now, suddenly, a lover's. Then he looked back at Hippolyta.

They stood there, each as still as the rock of Athens, staring at each other.

Yells erupted from both armies, cheering their heroes on.

'Hurry up, you idiots,' I muttered. 'If you don't move soon, the armies will charge.'

'Humans ...' Puck shook his head. 'It can take them years to recognise they've fallen in love.'

'Well, this pair had better do it quickly or their armies will be slashing at each other before you can say "honeysuckle wine"!'

Theseus and Hippolyta stepped forward. I couldn't tell who caught the other first, but I saw their lips meet. Her hands clutched at his back, then twined around him.

The armies stopped yelling faster than a pin can spear a butterfly. Silence fell like a cloak over the Athenian plain. Then suddenly both armies were cheering, everyone beating their spears or battle axes on their shields.

The Athenians' voices thundered across the plain. 'Theseus!'

'Hippolyta!' yelled the Amazons, just as loud.

The Amazons assumed Theseus had fallen so madly in love with their queen that he'd surrendered. The Athenians thought Hippolyta had been overcome with passion for their king. Both were pretty much the case, even if it was all thanks to me and the heartsease potion

Puck had taught me to make half a century or so ago. And Queen Titania too, because if she hadn't wanted a royal wedding to kick off her Midsummer Feast, Puck and I would never have come here.

Her Majesty's going to love this, I thought. Half the Amazons would be marrying Athenian men too, if I was any judge of the looks they were giving each other. Nothing like getting ready for a battle to get the hormones revved.

'Satisfied?' I enquired, handing the potion jar back to Puck.

'Quite satisfactory,' he said, making a note, then stuffing his quill and parchment and the jar under the belt of his breeches.

Some fairies would take credit for a stunt like this, but I knew Puck wouldn't. He'd make sure both King Oberon and Queen Titania knew that I'd been the one to plan it and then to pull it off.

Below us, Hippolyta and Theseus still embraced. The first of the Athenians and Amazons were slapping each other's backs in friendship. They'd be getting much closer than that soon enough.

'I'm off then,' I told Puck, and stretched myself back to full size. No one in either army would bother to look upwards just now, not with all those hormones, not to mention controlling war horses who couldn't understand why there'd been no battle.

Puck, still tiny, peered up at me. His wings were a bright satisfied purple now the job was done. 'Where are you off to, boy?'

'Dinner.'

'There's roast gryphon at the court tonight. Sweet Pea and Peach Fuzz and I thought we'd have a Dew Brew or two. Like to join us?'

There was always roast gryphon and Dew Brew at the Fairy Court. Fairies are conservative. And Sweet Pea and Peach Fuzz were as old as Puck.

'I was thinking of something a bit … wilder,' I said.

Puck grinned. 'Maybe after dinner we could get some travellers lost in the wood, or sour a cow's milk or something.'

That would be a real rambling rose of an evening, I thought. But I didn't say it aloud. I wanted that promotion.

Besides, I'd had enough of roast gryphon, dandelion salad and candied violets, not to mention fairy bread. There probably hadn't been a menu change at the Fairy Court for ten thousand years.

'Sorry. Got to go,' I told Puck.

I clicked my fingers and instantly I was wearing jeans and a jacket loose enough to hide my wings.

I had a date with a pizza.

CHAPTER 2

It was useful being able to TAP forward in time ten thousand years and across half the planet before you could say, 'House Special, no anchovies.' Which was just what I intended to say. My mouth watered as I pictured the lovely gooey pizza, crisp crust light enough to fly without fairy wings, melting cheese oozing off the edges, a few basil leaves floating on top and the best chunky tomato sauce since ... since forever.

Lousy-looking pizza shop though. I emerged outside it in a cloud of cocoa vapour (TAPing always comes with the scent of chocolate). It stood on the corner of a busy ocean highway, with sandhills at its back and cheap motels as neighbours. Wooden blinds sagged at the dusty windows and there was rust on the roof. The Leaning

Tower of Pizza had been a deli once. Aside from the new name painted in wobbly words on the door, nothing had changed since those days. The two cats washing their paws on the window ledge looked battered enough to have grown up begging for smoked salmon leftovers.

I ignored the long line of hopeful customers outside waiting for a table, opened the door and pushed inside. I'd been smart enough to stop on the way, twist time back to three weeks ago and book a table for tonight.

The café was nothing special inside either. A worn wooden floor — the best you could say of it was that it was clean, as if washed by the waves twice a day. It even smelled slightly salty. The chairs and tables might have been made of driftwood, but every one of them was occupied — except the best one in the corner. I twirled the couple that occupied it into an alternative universe just long enough for them to finish their pizzas and wipe their mouths, then hurled them back again ... and sat down in their spot the moment they got up to pay.

'So you're back again,' the owner said to me. 'Hope your taste in pizza has improved.'

She was short and a bit stocky, with broad shoulders and long black hair tied back in a ponytail. Her eyes were the colour of a tropical lagoon, neither blue nor green but as deep as both, and she had a tattoo of seaweed around her neck and wore a dress that looked like it was made of old sailcloth. Her teeth were small and very white and slightly pointed.

'Tomato, cheese, capers and black olives,' I said. 'No anchovies.'

She glared at me with those sea-coloured eyes. 'Who's the chef here? The anchovies are the best bit.'

'Who's the customer here? Haven't you ever heard that the customer is always right?'

'No.' She looked puzzled, as if no one had ever argued with her before, then shrugged as if it wasn't worth arguing about.

Every male in the café sighed in adoration. And there were a lot of them. Every table was occupied by a man, all staring at her with lovesick eyes even while they bit into their pizzas. The few women in the room glared at the men they'd thought were their boyfriends till they came in here — with the exception of one or two who looked as lovelorn as the men.

The owner vanished into the kitchen. The customers sighed and went back to eating or glaring at their boyfriends. She was the reason why the pizza shop was always full of course, not to mention the line of customers waiting outside. And everyone but me had anchovies on their pizza.

I sat back and picked up the menu to choose dessert. Apple pizza with ice cream, peach pizza with ice cream, apricot pizza with ice cream … I sensed a theme.

Three minutes later, the owner was back, my pizza in her hands. They were small muscular hands, I noticed, with pearl pink nails that were extremely clean.

I tried a smile. 'That was quick.' I checked to see there were no anchovies. Excellent.

No smile back. 'You need a hot oven for good pizza. If the temperature's too low, you get a tough crust and slop on the top.'

'Thanks,' I said sincerely. 'I've always wondered how to make the perfect pizza crust.'

I took a bite and sighed. Rude waitress/chef/owner or whatever else she was, her attitude was worth it. This pizza was the best food in ten thousand years.

'Anything else you want to know?' she asked.

I met her eyes. Her green-blue eyes. They had a strange sparkle, like dew on new grass at sunrise, and her lashes looked as thick and soft as the hair on a baby unicorn's mane. Not that I was interested. I was getting married in three days' time.

'Yes,' I said. 'How come every man here is in love with you?'

That was why I'd come here the first time — I hadn't even known about the pizza then. The scent of love in this place was so thick you could spread it on a hunk of pizza crust and watch it drip off the sides. But it wasn't the same scent as our heartsease love potion. What was going on here? Puck had sent me to find out whether someone was smuggling love potion — it was a major problem we fairies tried to keep on top of. You could control whole armies with a few drops of love potion, as I'd done just this morning. And if I uncovered an illegal potion operation here, Oberon would make me Puck's partner at midsummer, not just his chief assistant.

I took another bite of my pizza and tried not to drool. 'Cat got your tongue?' I asked, wiping tomato sauce off my chin.

She glared at me. 'I make great pizza.'

'Sure, you do.' I'd have come back for the pizza even without the chance to catch some potion-smugglers. 'But what else brings all these customers here?'

We were a long way out of town here. And most of the customers were regulars.

The owner slowly sat down in the seat opposite me and stared at me thoughtfully.

Every lovelorn customer sighed in envy, then glared at me.

'Fair exchange,' she said at last. 'How come you're not in love with me? You tell me your secret, and I'll tell you mine.'

Trust me: try telling a girl 'I'm actually a fairy' and she'll laugh and demand to see your wings. And I wasn't taking my jacket off to show them to her, not where everyone could see me.

'Let's just say I'm different.'

She shrugged. 'I can deal with different.' She gazed at me a bit more, then seemed to come to a decision. 'I officially close at ten but there's a … special sitting at midnight. Think you can handle it?'

'How special?'

'Very special.'

Was the potion-smuggling happening at this midnight sitting? I imagined a whole bunch of potion-pushers setting out from different places across the city to converge on the Leaning Tower of Pizza.

'Special is my middle name,' I said. 'Count me in.'

She smiled. It was a bit like sunlight on early morning waves. 'It's a deal. You tell me your secret then, and you'll find out mine. Want to book a table?'

'As long as I don't have to eat anchovies.'

'Your loss. What name should I use for the booking?'

No way was I going to tell her my name was Peaseblossom. 'Pete,' I said.

'Interesting to meet you, Pete. My name's Gaela.'

She went to collect the money from some customers who'd finally stopped pretending they were still drinking their coffee and had got up to pay. They left with a sad, lovesick glance back at Gaela — and the next customers in line outside pushed through the door.

I turned back to my pizza and took a mouthful of melting cheese. It was just the right amount so it didn't swamp the crust, and Gaela had managed to get the taste of sunlight into it somehow. And no anchovies.

Yes, I'd be back at midnight.

CHAPTER 3

Things were buzzing back in Fairyland, ten thousand pairs of wings flapping through the palace glades — every spot for two kilometres upwards seemed full of fairies gossiping in whispers. I changed back into my official rose-petal kilt and daisy garland and settled at my desk in the office glade where Titania's staff were based.

'What's happening?' I asked Mustardseed quietly.

Mustardseed lowered his voice discreetly. 'His Majesty spent the morning yelling because Her Majesty won't give up the boy.'

I sighed. 'Nothing new then.'

Queen Titania had found herself a new pet — a human child she'd taken from his family. The King was jealous of the affection she lavished on the boy and had demanded she hand him over to join his own retinue. We common fairies got the heartsease potion when we married: no jealousy, no quarrels. Royalty didn't. Oberon and Titania were always bickering about something. The Fairy Godmothers' Regimental Advice Bureau had put out a bulletin warning everyone to be careful not to comment too loudly. No one wanted to spend the next century as a toad or sweeping up butterfly droppings.

'Good work on the Theseus wedding by the way,' Mustardseed added in his normal tone. 'Everyone's talking about it.'

'Thanks,' I said. I lowered my voice again. 'What does the boy say about being here?'

Mustardseed shrugged. 'Nothing,' he whispered. 'Every time he opens his mouth, Her Majesty shoves a sugarplum into it.'

'Poor kid,' I said.

Mustardseed stared at me. 'That boy has everything. The Queen dotes on him. King Oberon wants to train him as one of his attendants. Either way, the kid's got it made.'

'Yeah — everything except what he really wants,' I said softly.

'What else should he want?'

Pizza (no anchovies) instead of sugarplums perhaps? But I didn't say anything. In the Fairy Court you did what you were told and felt what you were told to feel, and if you didn't it was cockroach time. I got stuck into work instead, allocating tasks to my team so we'd be ready for the Midsummer's Eve revels.

'Mustardseed, could you see if the new potion flasks are ready yet?'

Potion flasks are harvested from unicorn horn and, trust me, unicorns are very attached to their horns, which means you can only buy them from their descendants, and every one of them costs at least a tonne of moss scraped from Arctic rocks at midnight in mid-autumn. But flasks are fragile and an apprentice potion-maker goes through a tray of flasks like a whirlwind in a dust-bunny factory.

'Moth, we need more heartsease, and get the right flower this time.'

Last time Moth had picked heliotrope, which sharpens the appetite. A mob of hungry unicorns battling for the last carrot when you're trying to negotiate a price for their ancestors' horns isn't something you want to see again. No way Moth was going to be making Fairy Class 1 any time this millennium.

'Cobweb, check the nectar supply for the feast. You know the vintage the Queen likes? Not too sweet.

'Marshmallow, the last lot of rose petals weren't fragrant enough. You need to go to Bulgaria, nineteenth century, spring time. Go for the rich pink floppy roses and make sure you bring at least ten baskets full.

'Right, who has the list of possible mortal lovers for *next* midsummer's wedding? And check their family backgrounds this time. You all remember the Romeo and Juliet disaster.' The midsummer wedding planner before me was still scuttling around the dustbins.

I was in the middle of balancing the weather patterns for Midsummer's Eve — you can't just click your fingers to get a balmy moonlit night — when *ping*! I found myself on the grass at Queen Titania's feet. The Fairy Queen didn't bother with any kind of advance warning or summoning — if she wanted you, you were there. Four hundred years of practice had me bowing the moment my feet touched the grass. I had a quick glance around. We weren't in Fairyland, but in a glade that looked pretty much like the country I'd just been in with Puck in Theseus's time. Yes, there was the fortress of Athens in the distance.

'Your Majesty's pleasure?' I asked quickly.

I hoped she might congratulate me on the Athenian job, say something like 'Jolly good work, Peaseblossom'. I should have known better. Fairy royalty didn't do congratulations.

'Foot massage,' she said, and extended ten perfect bare toes. When you were Queen of the Fairies, you didn't need to bother with shoes, though she did wear flowers or silver lacing about her ankles sometimes.

I clicked my fingers. Puck's Massage Potion 59, heavy on the orange blossom with just a hint of mint, appeared in my hand. I opened the flask and began to rub the Queen's feet. Her Majesty ignored me as usual, staring instead at the magical image of the great hall of the Athenian court that was hovering above the glade. She was watching events the day after I'd enchanted Theseus and Hippolyta. I kept my eyes on my work. One pinched toe and Titania might have me polishing mushrooms for a decade.

Moth appeared next to me. He began to brush her hair, twining moonbeams between her locks to make them shine.

Queen Titania was beautiful. You got used to beauty at the Fairy Court — it's number one on the requirements to work there — but no one was as glorious as the Queen.

She was neither tall nor short, slim nor plump, but as soon as you looked at her you knew that everything about her — her height, her hair colour, whether sunrise red or moonrise gold — was exactly as beauty should be. Even her toenails were like pearls; or, rather, pearls were a dim reflection of Her Majesty's toenails.

I began on her other foot, into the swing of it now, and felt safe enough to look at what the Queen was watching.

Up in vision of the Athenian palace Theseus was smiling lovingly at Hippolyta, who was dressed in conventional women's clothes today. She looked a bit awkward, as if she was still learning not to trip over the long skirt. Even the way she walked was different — small steps in sandals instead of long strides in soft leather boots.

Theseus wore a leather kilt (a definite improvement on rose petals) and a crown had replaced his war helmet. He smiled at Hippolyta as he said, 'Now, fair Hippolyta, our nuptial hour draws on apace; two happy days bring in another moon. But, O, methinks, how slow this old moon wanes! She lingers my desires, like to a step-dame or a dowager long withering out a young man's revenue.'

I sighed. Kings, queens and aristocrats — they all love to declaim, mostly because no one dares tell them,

'Enough!' At least Theseus'd had the sense not to make a long speech on the battlefield. You should have heard Henry V, not to mention Caesar, Julius.

Hippolyta, however, seemed enchanted by the speech. I wondered what she would have thought of it without the heartsease potion. Amazon warriors weren't noted for their love of flowery declamations.

Titania laughed. 'Poor butterfly humans. Their lives are so short, and yet their flutterings can be amusing while they last.'

Three men entered the Athenian great hall to join the group of petitioners: a young man in a finely woven cream tunic who looked around as if he was interested in the whole court, not just the King; another about the same age whose robe was rich with embroidery and magnificence; and an older man who looked vain enough to believe himself still a fine figure of a gentleman, ignoring his discontented wrinkles every time he looked into his polished bronze mirror. A girl followed the three men. She was quite pretty, and kept her eyes lowered meekly as a virtuous daughter should, but I detected a hint of steel in her — even though this scene was taking place a few millennia before steel was invented.

'Happy be Theseus, our renowned duke!' said the older man obsequiously, bowing stiffly with a courtier's flourish.

A fellow declaimer. He must be rich then.

Theseus smiled at him graciously. 'Thanks, good Egeus. What's the news with thee?'

The old man's frown lines deepened. 'Full of vexation come I, with complaint against my child, my daughter Hermia.' He waved an age-spotted hand towards the young woman.

Hermia kept her eyes on her feet. I suspected she'd probably perfected foot-watching over many years so she didn't have to look at her father.

Egeus beckoned to the guy in the 'hey, look, I'm rich and magnificent' robe. 'Stand forth, Demetrius. My noble lord, this man hath my consent to marry her.'

Mr Magnificent smirked. He'd probably been used to getting his own way since he first demanded honey cake from his nurse.

Egeus's tone changed as he addressed the other young man. 'Stand forth, Lysander.' He could have been speaking to a slug now, the kind you found when you'd already eaten half the lettuce. He lowered his voice, as if about to tell a horrific tale of shipwreck or tsunami.

33

'My gracious duke, this man has bewitched my child! You, you, Lysander, you have given her rhymes, and exchanged love-tokens with my child.'

Hermia glanced up at Lysander for only a second, but her expression was so full of love it could have circled the moon twice.

Lysander gave her the smallest of smiles, enough to say, 'Don't worry. I love you and I'll stand firm.'

Hermia gave a tiny nod back.

I hadn't helped Puck for half a century or so without being able to see the shape and colours of love. Potion-induced love was royal purple striped with gold; a regal love, and perfect. But you never knew what the love that grew between two people by itself would be like. No two were ever the same, though in my job you didn't get to see them much. The love between Hermia and Lysander felt as strong as a cord of stars.

Egeus was still wittering on … I mean declaiming. His daughter Hermia refused to marry Demetrius, the man her father had chosen for her. Worse! She dared to love Lysander. At last Egeus finished and looked around to make sure that everyone had admired his declamation. Someone clapped at the back of the court — probably one of his servants.

Theseus turned to the girl. 'What do you say, Hermia? Be advised fair maid: to you your father should be as a god. Demetrius is a worthy gentleman.'

'So is Lysander,' said the girl quietly. She glanced at Lysander again, and the stars that linked them glowed. She raised her eyes imploringly to King Theseus. 'I beseech Your Grace: what is the worst that may befall me if I refuse to wed Demetrius.'

The girl had courage, even if not enough sense to understand that, human or fairy, we did what our lords demanded, in both life and love.

Whenever I'd felt even a flicker of attraction towards another fairy, I'd kept well away from them in case I fell in love before Their Majesties chose a bride for me. Potion THEN love. It was a good clear system. No arguments, no indecision.

Hermia should never have listened to Lysander's first words of adoration. And yet I couldn't help feeling sorry for her. And almost envious of the unique colours of love that linked her to Demetrius. But only 'almost'. After all, I was going to experience perfect purple love for my whole life. Flossie and I would live in the second-best mushroom in the finest ring in Fairyland. The Colonel of the Fairy Godmothers lived just two mushrooms down.

Theseus shrugged, as if a girl's love meant less than the shine on his shield. It probably did, as a good shine could dazzle an opponent. 'Either you die, or you do without the society of men forever,' he informed Hermia. 'Can you endure the livery of a nun, forever locked up in a shady cloister, to live a barren sister all your life?' He smiled confidently, waiting for her to fold.

I tried to remember how the Athenians had put disobedient women to death in Theseus's day. Was it by stoning? No, I remembered, they walled them up in a cave.

Hermia's question showed that she'd already known this. She had just been hoping the King might offer mercy. All he had to do was say three words: 'Let Hermia choose.' But he wouldn't say them. What king would? What would the world be like if everyone was free to choose their own love, to follow their dreams, their notions of what was right and wrong, instead of obeying their masters?

Titania clapped her hands and laughed. 'Humans can be so droll, can't they?'

'Yes, Your Majesty,' we chorused, laughing obediently with her.

All except one member of her court, sitting so still I hadn't noticed him before. He was about four years old, with dark hair and dark eyes. Her Majesty had ordered him dressed in sunflower petals that suited his brown skin, and he sat on a silk cushion, but there were shadows behind his eyes. He looked around at us, as if wondering why we laughed, then looked uncomprehendingly at the screen showing the events taking place in ancient Athens.

Did the child remember his old life? I wondered. Puck was supposed to apply the drops of forgetfulness every time Her Majesty picked up another human pet, but I saw anguish in the small boy's eyes. Puck had probably forgotten again.

I glanced back at the Athenian court, where Lysander was accusing Demetrius of making love to a girl called Helena, and Theseus was still telling poor Hermia she had to marry Demetrius, become a nun, or die. I could feel the girl's desperation even from here, but she was standing firm.

'Just delicious,' said Titania dreamily, inspecting her newly massaged toes. 'All that lovely human emotion. And a girl daring to say "no" to both her king and her father! So entertaining and tragic!'

'No one would ever want to say "no" to you, Your Majesty,' I said loyally. Which was true, but only because none of us wanted to spend a hundred years as a cockroach.

She gave me a brief smile, then turned back to the screen.

I followed her gaze. Why did Egeus want his daughter to marry Mr Magnificent anyway? I wondered. Lysander seemed to be as rich as Demetrius and equally well-born, and he made Hermia happy. Lysander probably also knew how to take no for an answer when a woman said she didn't want him. Probably Egeus wanted Hermia to obey him just because he could insist on it. Men like Egeus viewed women as property; and he wanted to make sure he handed his daughter over to someone just like himself.

Puck fluttered into the glade, bowing perfectly, his wings pale blue. 'Your Beauteous Majesty, His Majesty King Oberon begs that you attend him.'

Titania snapped her fingers at the scene in Athens, then inspected her fingernails as it vanished. 'His Majesty King Oberon can go dine with Medusa if he thinks he's getting my pretty pageboy. You don't want to go with Oberon, do you, my sweetie?'

The child gave her a quick, obedient smile. 'No, Your Majesty.'

'You love your Fairy Queen, don't you?'

'Yes, Your Majesty.' He spoke in fairy tongue — at least Puck had remembered to give him that.

'Good boy,' the Queen said. 'You shall have another sugarplum. But I had better see my husband.'

Suddenly Titania was gone, and with her Moth and Puck and the rest of the attendants. I looked at the kid sitting alone on his cushion, chewing his sugarplum. Being human, he couldn't follow everyone else without magic help. I supposed the Queen would eventually remember where she'd left him and send someone to bring him to her.

I sat cross-legged next to the boy. 'What's your name?'

He swallowed his plum. 'Puppy. Or Pretty Boy.'

'I mean your real name. The one you had before you came here.'

He looked at me cautiously. 'I'm not supposed to remember that. It was all a dream.'

'What was your name in your dream then?' I asked quietly.

'Polchis,' he whispered.

'Did you dream anything else, Polchis?'

'My father was the werowance — the chief of all the chiefs,' he said, sadness shadowing his words. 'We had a fine house made of wood and bark, and we ate roasted buffalo and goose and corn. I ... I don't like sugarplums.'

'What about roast gryphon?' I began, but the boy vanished from the glade before I could finish. Her Majesty must have remembered him.

CHAPTER 4

I flew back to my office feeling vaguely disturbed. Of course the boy must be happy with the Queen, but I couldn't see Her Majesty gnawing on a cob of corn or allowing roasted buffalo. She hardly even touched the roasted gryphon at the banquets. Still, perhaps I could tactfully give her a dish of honeyed nuts for the boy, in the hope that he liked those better.

Moth was already at his desk.

'Midsummer's Eve revels update,' I ordered him. 'We've only three days to go!'

'The Flower Fairy Orchestra is ready. They're performing the same music as last midsummer.'

I nodded. Naturally. Nothing changes much in Fairyland.

'The "Waltz of the Flowers" first, followed by the "Dance of the Sugar Plum Fairy", and then Elvis singing "Love Me Tender".'

Puck had plucked Elvis out of the real world in the seconds before he'd been about to suffer a heart attack from eating too many fried banana and peanut butter sandwiches. Puck had left a life-like mannequin in Elvis's place. Or a dead-like one in this case.

'The first course will take place while we watch the wedding of Theseus and Hippolyta. Puck has approved the menu on Oberon's behalf.'

'Roasted gryphon,' I said resignedly. 'Dandelion salad. Nasturtiums stuffed with rosebuds and rosebuds stuffed with nasturtiums in a mild moonbeam sauce. Dew Brew. Sugarplums and sweetmeats and candied violets.'

Moth nodded. 'Your wedding is scheduled to take place before the dessert course, then Elvis will sing again. After that, Theseus has arranged a play to amuse the guests at his own wedding.'

'Excellent. Her Majesty and King Oberon may enjoy that too.'

'It doesn't seem to be a very ... good ... play,' Moth said tentatively.

I shrugged. 'They're only human. If it gets boring, Elvis can sing again. Oberon loves "Hound Dog". Let's see if we can have a look at the actors.'

I clicked my fingers to bring up the image of the Athenian court, but there was no sign of Theseus and Hippolyta or any actors. Instead, the young man Lysander was whispering with Hermia. I was about to fast-forward in time to see the play, but something in their faces stopped me. I saw a lot of love in my job, but not love freely chosen. Or a love strong enough to withstand threats of death. I turned up the volume.

Lysander held Hermia's hand and said softly, 'Hear me, Hermia.'

She nodded, drinking in the sight of him. Poor girl. If Theseus carried out his promise to wall her up in a cave if she refused to obey her father, her lover's face might be one of the last things she ever saw.

'I have a widow aunt, a dowager,' Lysander continued, 'wealthy, and with no children of her own. Her house is seven leagues away from Athens, and she thinks of me as her only son. There, gentle Hermia, may I marry you.' He gazed down at her. 'The sharp Athenian law cannot pursue us there,' he promised.

Hope lit Hermia's face like sunrise. Lysander was offering her not just life, but love too. Not to mention a rich marriage, though I doubted she cared for that.

Lysander lifted her hand to his lips and kissed it gently. 'If you love me, then creep from your father's house tomorrow night to the place in the wood, only a league beyond the town, where I met you with Helena once, on a morning in May. I'll wait for you there.'

'Oho,' said Moth, 'this is getting interesting. Do you think she'll do it?'

'Of course she will,' I said, just as Hermia began to speak, her voice choked with happiness.

'My good Lysander! I swear to you, by Cupid's strongest bow, by all the vows that ever men have broke (in number more than ever women spoke), in that same place that you have told me, tomorrow truly will I meet with thee.'

Now that's how you give a good declamation, I thought. Not too long, and from the heart.

Someone else was slipping into the Athenian hall.

Hermia looked around and smiled. 'Here comes Helena,' she said, and held her hand out to her friend.

The young woman had dark hair and a sulky mouth, but she smiled sweetly when Hermia explained that she was going to sneak out of her father's house to marry

Lysander, especially when Hermia pointed out that Demetrius, who for some off reason Helena found irresistible, would then be free to marry her.

'Well, that settles that,' said Moth, about to flick the image off as Hermia and Lysander left the hall. 'They're all going to live happily ever after.'

'No, stop,' I said. There'd been something about Helena's expression ...

Yes, I was right. Alone now, she was muttering how she'd tell Demetrius about Hermia eloping with Lysander so he could stop her. Demetrius would be so pleased with Helena that he'd ...

He'd what? I shook my head. Did Helena really believe that if Demetrius caught Hermia about to elope, he'd decide not to marry her and marry Helena instead? He already knew that Hermia hated him and loved Lysander, yet he'd still agreed to marry her. Why would anything Helena told him change his mind?

'Helena's not very bright, is she?' Moth said. 'If she just left everything alone, Hermia would be gone and Demetrius might actually marry her without any need for further plotting.'

'Dumb as a damp duckling,' I agreed, turning the volume down. 'Fine husband he's going to make.'

Moth handed me a sheet of parchment covered with a long numbered list in neat writing. 'Speaking of husbands, the Fairy Floss has sent some suggestions for your own wedding.'

'Who? Oh, right. Okay, let's see them.' I ran my eyes down the parchment. Attendants wearing white rose-petal tunics trimmed with milk teeth … an arch of Assistant Tooth Fairies holding up their pliers. I knew that sometimes teeth need a bit of encouragement to shift but I was sure the pliers would be clean and shining for the wedding arch.

'Fair enough,' I said.

'Yes, she'll be conducting the ceremony.'

'Who?'

'Fairy Nuff. Then a white butterfly will arrive to carry you off on your honeymoon. The Fairy Floss has booked a foxglove in Wollongong, Australia.'

'Wollongong, Australia? Has she got a thing about kangaroos or something? Why Australia?'

'Apparently there's going to be a dentists' convention on at the same time.'

I'd never been to a dentists' convention, and even after I'd been made to fall in love with Flossie completely and forever, I suspected I still wouldn't want to go to one.

But seeing her happy would make me happy — that was just one of the many good things about unconditional, absolutely forever, potion love. And I could just TAP off while Flossie was listening to a lecture on extracting wisdom teeth and grab a pizza somewhere.

'Look.' Moth pointed to the image of Athens. The scene had changed. Some figures wearing tatty tunics lounged around a small room in what looked like a labourer's home instead. 'Those must be the actors for King Theseus's play.' He consulted another piece of parchment. 'That one's Quince, then there's Snug, Bottom, Flute, Snout and Starveling.'

I sniggered. 'You're joking?'

Moth shook his head. 'True as I'm fluttering here. Theseus must have employed every actor with a rude name in Athens. Except Quince isn't a rude word.'

'It was back then,' I said. 'It was another word for breasts. As for Flute and Snout ...' I shook my head and peered at the would-be actors as they discussed their play. 'Bottom sounds like an idiot.'

'He's a weaver,' said Moth, as if that explained it.

I flicked off the image and we bent to our work again. The midsummer revels took weeks to organise, and the last-minute details could be murder. It was six hours before I'd got through all the paperwork on my desk. Or rather, six hours by the watch I'd forgotten to take off when I came back from the Leaning Tower of Pizza. No time ever really passed in Fairyland.

I reckoned I'd earned a break. Theoretically fairies didn't get time off, but when you could split time, stop time, or make it sit up and miaow like a kitten, it was easy enough to find some just for yourself. Most of us had hobbies. Moth and Cobweb liked the dragonfly races; Puck enjoyed turning milk sour and beer flat.

For me, it was pizza. And, just now, one pizza shop in particular and possibly a chance to break up a potion-smuggling ring and get two promotions instead of one.

CHAPTER 5

Jeans back on, wings tucked in, the scent of choc-coated sultanas all around me, I sauntered into the Leaning Tower of Pizza. There was no line of customers outside, but even though it was just on midnight, inside it was just as crowded as earlier, except for two tables with a Reserved sign on them — one a singleton, the other set for six. I sat at the small table and looked around. The clientele was ... different.

I picked up the menu. Same cover. Different pizzas. 'Dead Delicious' was probably what the guy with grey skin — well, bits of skin — and black hollows where his eyes had been was eating. 'Billy Goat's Gruff, with Cheese and Anchovies' would suit the table of trolls over in the corner; while the pack of werewolves were probably tearing into 'Road Kill with Anchovies'. And 'Snot, Anchovies and Englishmen' was obviously meant for the giant sitting cross-legged on the floor, his head brushing the ceiling.

Despite the change in clientele, they were all still looking longingly at Gaela, when they weren't glaring at each other. Except for a pair of banshees holding what were probably hands — it was hard to tell with banshees — across the table and feeding each other bits of pizza. True love, I thought, looking at their glow of orange, gold and black, and strong enough to withstand whatever else was going on here.

Gaela slid a pizza that seemed to be topped with flies, anchovies and cheese in front of what might be a bunyip if anyone could get a good look at him. The wombat next to him ... or her ... or it ... was munching its way through what the menu listed simply as 'Carrot Pizza with Carrot'.

Gaela made her way over to me. 'Well?' she demanded.

'House Special again. No dead flies, no road kill, no anchovies. What's a wombat doing here among all the fey?'

'The bunyip doesn't like to eat alone. You said you'd explain why ...' Gaela left the rest unsaid.

'Why I'm not madly in love with you?'

She nodded.

'You said you'd explain,' I waved a hand around, 'all this.'

It still wasn't making sense. Trolls and bunyips weren't potion-pushers.

'All right. But not in here.' Gaela glanced at her customers, but everyone still had a plate full of pizza. Of course they had. Except for the banshees, they'd been too busy staring at her with lovesick eyes to eat.

'Follow me. I've got a delivery to make,' said Gaela shortly. She led the way over to the door into the kitchen.

Every person — and every werewolf or troll — except for the banshees watched me enviously as I followed her through the door and shut it behind me. It was quite a kitchen. Well-scrubbed wooden walls, tiled floor, stainless-steel table and benches, and a giant pizza oven with a neat stack of driftwood beside it. So that was what gave the pizzas their salty tang, I realised the scent of the sea.

Ingredients were neatly lined up on one bench — slugs, road kill and so on in labelled and sealed containers; rocket, grated cheeses, three kinds of sliced mushrooms, sliced cooked potatoes and all the rest in their containers too. There was no sign of any illegal potion flasks.

On the other bench were small balls of pizza dough waiting to be stretched flat and loaded with toppings. I shut my eyes and imagined eating the House Special all over again, no anchovies.

'Which is your favourite?' I asked, my eyes still closed.

'Anchovy, cheese and caramelised onion.'

I opened my eyes. 'I don't like anchovies.'

'I guessed,' said Gaela dryly.

I looked at the whiteboard that listed the various combinations. I hadn't tried most of them yet.

'Sweet potato, fetta and rocket,' I read aloud. 'Doesn't the rocket shrivel in the oven?'

'I scatter it on top as soon as the pizza comes out of the oven, and the fetta gives off enough steam to wilt it.'

'Tomato, black olives, mozzarella ...'

'Classic but excellent,' said Gaela. 'I use half fresh skinned tomatoes and half homemade tomato sauce.'

'Artichoke, eggplant, tomato and three cheeses?'

'The artichoke has to be just firm enough to give some bite. That's the secret of pizza — thin crust, thin topping, something soft, something firm, something sweet and something acidic, and all with a touch of salt. There are thousands of possible combinations.'

'Why don't you let your customers choose their toppings then?'

'Because they'd probably choose wrong. And anyway, they don't want to. Customers like a nice uncomplicated menu where they don't have to do too much thinking. Like the customer you're about to meet now.'

She picked up the largest pizza box I'd ever seen, wrapped it in a waterproof cloth, then opened the back door. A gust of ocean wind sent the fire flickering in the back of the oven.

'Oh,' I said, as everything became clear.

The kitchen door didn't open onto sandhills as I'd expected. The café must have been built between them, because two steps down and my feet met a beach. White sand glowed as gold in the moonlight as the cheese on Gaela's pizzas, smoothed by the retreating tide. Waves tumbling in neat rows of three, as if someone had crocheted their white tops. The scent of seaweed, and a horizon where the dark sea ruffled and met the star-dusted sky.

Gaela turned to me and laughed, the lacy waves already nibbling at her toes. She put the pizza down on the sand out of the waves' reach and pulled her sack-like dress over her head. She wore nothing underneath it.

She untied her ponytail, strode into the waves, then dived down. She came up, wet face glowing. And suddenly she wasn't a sour-faced pizza chef. She wasn't even human.

'You're a selkie,' I said slowly.

Gaela laughed again, her true self here in the water.

No, I thought, Gaela *is* a pizza chef — no one could cook like that and not be a chef to the heart — but she was a selkie too, and that was why her customers adored her. There was no illegal potion racket going on here. Every mortal man — and also zombies, trolls and even bunyips, it seemed — had to love a selkie as soon as she took on a human shape.

Even as I looked, Gaela changed. She dived down and a shining black seal splashed up instead, plunging and leaping all around me. I didn't need to hear her voice to know she was laughing again. Seal or human, she was the most beautiful creature I had ever seen. But I was not in love with her. Selkie magic didn't work on fairies.

I wasn't in love with her even when she took human form again, the water dripping off her silken skin that glowed in the moonlight.

She strode out of the water, still naked, and picked up the waterproofed pizza box. 'I need to make that delivery. Coming in?'

'I can't swim,' I said.

'What!' She made it sound as if I had to live within a shoebox. 'Not at all?'

I shook my head and took off my hoodie. The sea breeze felt chilly on my wings as they unfolded. I shook them to get rid of the crumples and felt a tongue of moonlight stroke them. Wings were more sensitive than skin.

'I see,' she said slowly. 'You're a fairy. Magic doesn't work on you.'

'Not selkie magic. Or leprechaun tricks or vampire glamour or elf magic. Only our own kind.'

'That's why you're not in love with me then, like all the other customers are.'

I nodded. 'That's why I can't swim either. The wings get in the way. Plus, if your wings get sodden, you can't fly till they dry out.'

Even if they were slightly damp, it would take me longer than the split microseconds allowed to get back to the Fairy Court when Their Majesties called me, though I didn't tell Gaela that.

She grinned. 'You haven't lived till you've seen the world below the water. Sand-strewn caverns, cool and deep, where the winds are all asleep. I saved a shipwrecked poet called Arnold once — he talked about it like that. "Wild white horses foam and fret" — that was in a storm. Down in the sea you can feel every creature near you move in the caress of the water on your skin. Air is so ... so dull in comparison.'

'But you run a pizza shop!'

'Yep. I make pizza *and* I swim. And you can too. Anyone can swim with a selkie,' she added as I began to protest again. 'How else can we rescue shipwrecked sailors or lure fishermen into the waves?'

'But my wings ...'

'They'll dry! I can even lend you a hairdryer.'

She stretched her hand out to me. Such a firm hand, muscular from kneading dough, slightly webbed between the fingers. Her fingernails shone like pearls.

For a moment I was tempted. I looked at the moon's gold highway across the water — what *would* it be like down there? Did moonbeams dance in water as sunbeams did in air? And if Her Majesty did call me, I could use the hairdryer on my wings and then cut time even finer. Titania would never notice.

I felt my hand reach for hers. Our fingers touched. Hers were cool from the water yet warm at the same time.

I quickly pulled my hand back and thrust it safely behind me, away from temptation. 'Not tonight,' I said.

Even a wet mist slowed a fairy down to the speed of sound. I needed to be able to flash back to the Fairy Court as soon as I was called. I couldn't risk experimenting with hairdryers, not so close to the Midsummer's Eve revels. Or that's what I told myself.

Gaela stared at me for a long moment, her expression hard to read. Was that wistfulness? And was it for me, or for her?

She plunged into the water again. For a few seconds I saw her pale shape spearing through the ripples, then she dived, still holding the pizza. My gaze swept the ocean, all black and gold and starlight, but there was no sign of her.

Suddenly something reared up in the moonlight, first one great coil, and then another, and finally a head like a tyrannosaurus on steroids, with a tail lashing at least a hundred metres behind. A sea serpent!

I knew they were immortal, like fairies and selkies, elves, leprechauns and vampires. The famous Loch Ness serpent must have been around for at least two million years. Selkie magic wouldn't work on a sea serpent. In fact, a selkie might just be a crunchy snack for a sea serpent.

The massive mouth opened, showing fangs a sabre-toothed tiger would envy. And there was Gaela again, treading water just below it, her dark hair plastered to her back.

I had maybe three seconds to save her. Or less. But if I moved now, I could cut time. Once she'd been eaten, there was nothing I could do. I couldn't change the past unless I'd already been there.

I spread my wings ... then stopped as Gaela held up the pizza box, completely unfazed by the monstrous beast towering above her. She carefully opened the lid. The serpent bent its head so Gaela could feed it the first slice.

A strange shiver ran through the waves, as if they were flirting with the sand.

The sea serpent was purring.

CHAPTER 6

The serpent took its time eating. I supposed after a hundred millennia diet of fish and the odd human, pizza tasted incredible. Especially Gaela's pizza. I wondered what sea serpents liked on their pizzas.

Gaela trod water patiently, lifting up each slice, sea serpents being lacking in the hands department. The big beast took each piece from her hand as neatly as a kitten licking from a bowl. Finally it finished. Its tongue came out, vast enough to carpet Theseus's palace. It licked its lips, fossicking for every crumb or scent of cheese and tomato.

And then it dived, head first, followed by the massive ridges of its body. It reared up once more with what was probably a thank-you grin upon its giant face —

it was hard to tell — and a bundle suspended from its teeth.

Gaela reached up and took the bundle, then plunged down into the ocean. The sea serpent did that 'maybe it's a grin' again, and then it vanished too, causing more ripples than the sinking *Titanic*.

I knew Gaela would be back. Even now she might be swimming towards me, in seal shape perhaps, past those sand-strewn caverns she'd mentioned, below the white froth of waves.

I sat down on the sand, the stars glimmering above me, brighter than any I'd ever seen before, the wind tasting of salt and fresh bread and something new too. In all my four hundred years I had never seen anything as beautiful as Gaela feeding pizza to the serpent, her skin the colour of the moonlight, the serpent's scales gleaming like the stars.

There was nothing wrong with admiring beauty, I told myself. This breathless feeling, like I'd been punched in the stomach, was because it had been so lovely. Plus admiration for anyone, human or selkie, who could make the best pizza in the world; pizza that could even entice a serpent near the shore.

'And I'm getting married,' I muttered to myself.

After Midsummer's Eve, I'd be in love for the rest of my life with the most efficient Tooth Fairy who'd ever held a pair of pliers — according to Puck, who'd known a lot of them. I'd be happy forever.

Gaela emerged from the waves in front of me, human-shaped, laughing from the sheer joy of water, waves and the serpent's delight in the best pizza in the universe, her body dappled with starlight reflected in the drops of sea water that clung to her bare skin. She held a dripping bag in one hand.

Selkie magic doesn't work on fairies, I reminded myself as I tossed her the sack dress, and waited while she put the bag down and slipped the dress back on. Focus, Peaseblossom! You're getting married!

Gaela stopped, the dress suspended above her head. 'What did you just say?' she demanded.

Had I said that aloud?

'I'm … getting married on Midsummer's Eve,' I said firmly.

She carefully lowered her dress over her body and pushed her wet hair behind her ears. The laughter had left her. She didn't look at me, and I tried not to look at her. I would probably never see a selkie again, and if I did, it wouldn't be Gaela.

Finally she glanced at me again. 'Aren't you a bit young to be getting married?' she asked.

I shrugged. 'I'm four hundred and six. How old are you?'

'Four hundred and one,' she admitted.

'You're right, four hundred is a bit young to be married. But when Queen Titania says you're getting married, you don't argue.'

'Your queen chose your bride for you?'

'Of course. It's ... tidier that way. No distractions, like spending forever looking for your soul mate, or checking each other out over a cup of Dew Brew. Anyway, a few drops of heartsease potion and I'll love whoever Her Majesty chose for me all my life.'

More silence.

Gaela strolled out of the shallows and sat on the sand next to me. I pulled my hoodie back on, glad I was in jeans and not a rose-petal kilt.

'What's her name?' she asked finally. 'The fairy you're marrying?'

'What?' I'd been thinking how the moon somehow looked twice as bright tonight. And how Gaela had looked in the water, as if the waves were laughing with her. And how sitting so close to her I could smell her scent — seaweed, salt and warm pizza crust. 'Her name's Floosie. I mean Flossie. The Fairy Floss, First Assistant Tooth Fairy for the entire north-west region.'

'North-west of where?'

'Does it matter?'

Flossie and I would both be promoted after our wedding. I'd be Puck's permanent assistant, first in line for his job when he retired. Flossie would be Chief Regional Tooth Fairy. In a hundred years or so we would be the most important fairies of the court, Chief Tooth Fairy and Chief Potion Fairy, reporting directly to King Oberon and Queen Titania.

'No, it doesn't matter at all,' Gaela said slowly. Her expression was impossible to read. 'I'm getting married too. Soon.'

Why did I suddenly feel like a wave had slapped my face?

'That's nice,' I managed to say. 'Especially as he'll have to love you forever too, you being a selkie. It's … it's good to have these things sorted out in advance — to know you'll never quarrel and there's no chance of ever falling out of love. No messiness …' My voice died away at the contempt in her face.

Gaela lifted her chin. Her seaweed tattoo glowed in the moonlight. 'Magic!' She almost spat the word.

'I wouldn't use enchantment on someone I love, especially to make them marry me. Guyye's like you — selkie magic doesn't affect him.'

'He's a fairy too?'

Impossible, I thought. No fairy would disobey Oberon and Titania, and they'd never give a fairy permission to marry a selkie. And if any fairy had even tried, I'd have heard the gossip.

'Guyye's not a fairy,' she said.

'A leprechaun?' I asked incredulously.

Some of my best friends were leprechauns. Well, we'd been out partying a few times. But leprechauns were small and green, and Gaela was ... Gaela, whether in human form or seal.

She laughed. 'No.'

'An elf?' I kept my voice cautious. It was never a good idea to offend an elf and they took offence easily. Just say something offhand like, 'Feeling a little down tonight, are we, short stuff?' and you might find an elf punching your kneecap.

'Not an elf.' Gaela's voice softened. 'Guyye's the most wonderful man I've ever met. He's ... powerful. Other men just moon about, living day after day all the same, never thinking that their lives might be different. Guyye *does* things. He makes things happen.'

Don't let the curls and fairy wings fool you; I'd worked out since I was a hundred and four. But powerful wasn't just about muscles. Not the way Gaela said it. Powerful meant charisma.

Fairies have many excellent attributes — beds made of foxgloves, and mushroom cottages, and fairy wands that can turn pumpkins into coaches and mice into confused coachmen, not to mention fairy dust as long as you aren't allergic to it — but charisma isn't one of them.

'Was Guy at the café this afternoon or tonight?' I asked.

I hadn't noticed any particularly wonderful guys among the customers. Besides, every one of them, except a few affronted girlfriends, the banshees and the wombat, had been in enchanted love with Gaela. You couldn't be assistant to Puck for almost fifty years without being able to sense enchantment.

'His name is Guyye, not Guy. Two *y*s and an *e*. Guyye can only come out at night — that's why I have the second sitting at midnight. But I don't mind. Selkies love the moonlight.' And suddenly I knew, even before she added, 'Guyye's a vampire.'

Gaela scrambled to her feet, then picked up the bag the sea serpent had given her. 'He should be here by now. Something must have kept him. I'll introduce you.'

I'd rather have ridden a slug through the city centre in my rose-petal kilt. Instead, I smiled politely and said, 'Love to. What's in the bag?'

'Anchovies and sardines. I swap them for pizza.'

She opened the door into the kitchen. The oven fire still glowed just the same, and when we went back into the main room no one seemed to have eaten much pizza, great as it was. I suspected that time in the sea with a selkie could be folded just like fairy time.

But a little time must have passed, because the larger reserved table that had been empty now had a customer. And he wasn't eating pizza.

Guyye was every vampire cliché you've ever seen: tall, dark, handsome, pale skin, black eyes that seemed to see into the heart of you and count each red corpuscle.

Gaela made her way between the tables. I followed her more slowly. The customers were staring as though they couldn't work out who they were most drawn to, him or her.

Selkie magic doesn't work on vampires. But vampire charisma works on everyone. Even I felt it, and I'd been inoculated by many years of love-potion fumes. Surely Gaela must know that Guyye's charisma was working on her too?

I glanced at her. Gaela wasn't thinking of anything but him.

'Guyye,' she said breathlessly.

Guyye smiled with just a hint of fang. 'Sorry I didn't get here earlier, babe. People to do, things to see, that kind of thing.'

'Of course.' Gaela remembered my existence. 'Guyye, this is Pete.'

He extended a hand to shake, long and white-fingered and strong enough to break every bone in mine. 'Pete. O-positive, my favourite flavour.'

Gaela smiled. I didn't.

'Only joking,' Guyye added.

'Of course,' I said politely.

'Guyye and I are going to run the Leaning Tower of Pizza together after we're married,' said Gaela adoringly. 'He's thinking of franchising. He loves pizza as much as I do.'

A vampire who loved pizza? At least selkies and fairies could eat pizza, even if Gaela was the first selkie to make it. But vampires only ate one thing, and it didn't come with cheese. Or anchovies.

Guyye had hold of Gaela's hand now and was kissing it from fingertip to wrist, which was about forty-nine kisses too many for a pizza parlour. He didn't bother looking at me again. I doubted he'd really noticed me at all, not with that O-positive crack. Fairies were all AB-negative. If he'd paid any attention, he'd have known it.

But this was Gaela's choice, I reminded myself. It had nothing to do with me. I was getting married very soon myself. I had no right to even think about interfering in her life …

'What does a vampire want with a pizza parlour?' I asked.

Guyye stopped kissing Gaela and finally looked at me. 'Oh, I have my reasons.'

'I'm sure you have. What are they?'

Guyye gave me a quick glimpse of fang. It didn't bother me. I supposed a vampire could blood-suck a fairy, but not if the fairy made himself mosquito-sized. Too small to bite, too fast to fight, and a buzzing mosquito annoyed even vampires. Cobweb and I had found that out when we were joking around as kids.

'Well?' I demanded.

Guyye ignored me, picking up Gaela's hand and giving it another licking. Given where those lips had been, I couldn't say I'd have wanted them on me. Nor would Gaela if she was in her right mind.

'Can't stay, babe,' Guyye said, with what she obviously assumed was regret. 'Got a meeting.' He tapped his nose. 'Big doings.'

'Of course. I understand.' Gaela couldn't quite hide her disappointment. 'I just hoped we could look at the wedding menu this evening.'

Now *that* would be interesting. Pizza and bridesmaids for the main course perhaps? The flower girl for an entrée? And probably not a church wedding, in case the groom, his family and friends all burst into flames.

Guyye smiled at Gaela with extra wattage, giving off so much charisma that even I felt a twinge. 'I'll see you tomorrow night, babe. It'll be a big one, so make sure you put the Closed sign up early. One special sitting only. I've got every table booked for you.'

'Thank you.' Gaela's voice sounded like a little girl's thanking someone for a lollipop.

'You have every table filled every night,' I pointed out.

Guyye looked at me as if I were a tomato: fat, red and juicy but of no interest to a vampire. 'Not with people who matter.'

'Everyone matters,' I said, annoyed, then realised he was right. Because of course some people mattered more than others. That was the way the world was made. And Fairyland as well. Titania and Oberon mattered more than all of the rest of us put together. Hippolyta and Theseus mattered more than any of the others in ancient Athens. Puck mattered more than the thousands of fairies who spend their nights putting dew on rosebuds or polishing rainbows. Or doing a tonne of paperwork for the Midsummer's Eve revels …

'It will be a wonderful night,' Gaela said softly. 'I'll make sure it's perfect. I've even had a new idea for the tomato sauce —'

'Just be yourself, babe. That's all we need.' Guyye made another slow detour of her wrist, kissing his way up her arm, then stood and kissed her briefly on the cheek. 'Till tomorrow night, darling.'

'Till tomorrow night,' Gaela said breathlessly.

She watched him go, striding out as if he owned the place. Which he would, of course, after the wedding.

The other customers looked relieved to have only one

person in the room to be devoted to again. They even managed to eat some pizza.

The bunyip and the wombat stood up to pay. I waited till Gaela had processed their credit cards, then sat down at the free table. I was the only diner without a pizza, I realised, till I saw Gaela was carrying one over to me. What a girl. Or selkie.

She waited till I'd taken my first bite — plenty of tomato, a small scattering of cheese, tiny black olives, and a few sliced artichokes with just enough crunch to be perfect — then sat down next to me.

'It's wonderful, isn't it?' she said softly.

I nodded. 'There's something about the crust. How do you keep it thin but light and moist at the same time?'

'I meant love,' she said. 'As for the crust — I let the dough rise slowly for twenty-four hours, use a high-gluten flour and sea water. Sea water is full of minerals, so the crust stays firm despite the softness of the gluten.'

I put the slice down. 'Gaela, you're four hundred years old. You have to know about vampires. They enchant their prey.'

She glared at me. 'I'm not stupid. But Guyye's never laid a fang on me.'

'They like to play with their food too.'

She stood up. 'If that's all you've got to say …'

'I'm sorry. Sit down.'

She hesitated, then sat.

'Why does he want to marry you?' I asked.

Her glare grew as hot as melted cheese. 'Is it so impossible that someone should love me? Really, truly love me, without selkie enchantment?'

'Of course not. You're beautiful. Not that it matters to me,' I added hurriedly. 'I'm getting married soon myself. But vampires usually don't go in for all that love stuff.'

'Known many vampires, have you?'

I shook my head. The only vampires I'd met were the ones Cobweb and I had buzzed, and that was just a quick zoom in and out. Fairies and vampires kept pretty much to themselves. Most of what I knew about them came from —

'Books and movies,' said Gaela disgustedly. 'You've absorbed a pile of species-ist clichés. Doesn't the fact that Guyye wants to marry me prove that vampires can love?'

'Maybe,' I admitted. 'But why do you want to marry him? Apart from him being tall, dark and handsome, irresistible and never needing to use curl-taming conditioner,' I added quickly.

Her look softened. 'Because he loves my pizza shop too.'

'I like your pizza shop. You have a whole café full of customers who adore your pizza shop.'

'That's just selkie charm,' she said dismissively.

'Trust me, you make the best pizza in ten thousand years. Even if you weren't a selkie, your café would still be full. And you know it.'

'I know my pizza is good,' she said. 'It has to be, so I can be sure people are coming for it not just because of the magic. But loving pizza isn't the same as wanting to run a pizza shop. Have you ever heard of a selkie running a pizza shop?'

'No.'

'No one else has either. I'm the first selkie who's ever made pizza. Some selkies choose to live on the land with fishermen for a few years, but that's not the same as running a business. My family disowned me when I opened this place. None of my so-called friends has even been here.' She added bitterly, '"Go and lure a few fishermen instead," they told me. "Sing prophecies from the waves. Rescue shipwrecked sailors and leave them on the sand."'

'Rescuing sailors is a good thing to do,' I said.

'Yes, but it's not what I want to do with my life. And,' she said defiantly, 'my pizzas *are* good. It took me years to perfect that crust, to find exactly the right cheeses, to experiment with which toppings work together. I don't think anyone else has ever made Gouda, potato and black olive pizza, but it *works*, just like sardine and potato are brilliant together too. No cheese, just really thick tomato sauce. And Guyye is the first person —'

'Vampire.'

'First *person* who has ever taken me and my pizzas seriously. I'm more than selkie enchantment to him. I'm … I'm *me*!' Her blue-green eyes had a challenge in them now. 'And you know what? I don't care if Guyye *has* used charisma on me. He loves me and I love him and we're going to live our own life together. No enchanting fishermen, no bat-infested castles with a coffin in the dungeon. Just the two of us together, making the best pizza in the world.'

'And it doesn't matter that you might only love his vampire glamour?'

'No. Love is love, isn't it? He's right for me, and I am for him.'

I didn't have anything to say to that. I ate another slice of pizza instead.

The trolls got up to pay, and then the banshees too, still hand in hand. It was usually chilly near a banshee —

if you ever get a shiver down your spine and don't know why, a banshee may be close by — but tonight the air about them was as warm as a spring breeze. I could almost smell rose blossom.

But it was nearly dawn — time for the banshees to howl on the rooftops of all the souls who would die today. And as the sun swung up above the horizon, Guyye would need to take shelter from the daylight …

'What about you?' Gaela asked, interrupting my thoughts.

'What do you mean?'

'You and this Fairy Floss. You don't seem to mind that your love is going to be caused by enchantment.'

'Love is love,' I repeated slowly. Puck even had the creed on a placard in his potion lab.

'So why are you worrying about me and Guyye?' She smiled, and suddenly it was as if the moon shone through the café ceiling. 'You'll be married, and Guyye and I will be married and making the best pizza in the world. You can bring your Fairy Floss here. Does she like pizza?'

'I don't know,' I admitted.

'What do you do for a job anyway?'

'Me personally? Mostly enchant people Their Majesties think should fall in love.'

I didn't mention the paperwork or the foot massages, but there'd be less paperwork and hopefully no foot massages after I was married and had been promoted.

'There you are then,' Gaela said. 'It doesn't really matter why people love each other as long as they do.' She yawned and looked around the café. The last customers were finally finishing their pizzas. 'I'd better get some sleep. I have to get up mid-afternoon to light the oven, then bring up the driftwood.' She dimpled. 'A couple of mermen collect it for me. They love black olives on their pizza. Olives are impossible to get in the sea unless a ship with a decent dining room sinks.'

'Where do you sleep?' I asked. I hadn't seen a door that might lead to a bedroom.

'In the waves.' She smiled again and I could almost see the sunrise in it. 'I'm still a selkie, after all. What about you?'

'I sleep in a foxglove flower. It's traditional.'

She stared, obviously comparing my height with a foxglove.

I flicked myself tiny, then full-sized again. 'See? I can be whatever size I want to be.'

'Useful.'

'Saves on rent.' Not to mention that at the size I was now I'd need slightly over a million rose petals on my kilt to stay decent.

'There's a whole foxglove glade for us fairy bachelors,' I told her. 'It's a bit cramped, to be honest, no matter what size I am. But after we're married, Flossie and I will move into our own mushroom in a fairy ring near Their Majesties.'

I was looking forward to the mushroom — it got chilly in a foxglove flower, and there's hardly any room for bookcases. Our mushroom was white with red spots and an attractive tilt to the roof, with red and white curtains at the first- and second-floor windows, a bright red door and wooden shutters on the attic. It was right next-door to Puck's mushroom and almost the same size too, with two bathrooms plus an ensuite, a small library, a mini gym, a potion parlour for me, and a tooth display room for Flossie where she could keep her prize samples; and a childcare centre just across the ring for when Their Majesties decided we should have children. The ring even had its own fairy piper at dawn and dusk, and its cobwebs came pre-jewelled. It was wonderful, far more spacious and polished than the Leaning Tower of Pizza, so I didn't know why I felt sort of —

'And you'll be happy,' said Gaela slowly.

I nodded. 'Just as happy as you'll be with Guyye.'

And she would be happy. Besides, it was in no way my business, whereas making sure these particular Midsummer's Eve revels were the best ever definitely *was* my business. But I still hesitated.

'Can I book a table for tomorrow night?' I asked.

It would mean I'd need to stretch time to fit in two extra nights, just at my busiest, but what else was TAP for? Besides, I was curious about who these important people were. Plus, with all the extra work to organise the revels, I deserved a decent pizza before my wedding I told myself.

And, okay, I was really worried for Gaela. Just as a friend, of course. There was no reason why fairy fiancés couldn't have friends, even if they were female and a selkie. But there was something here that smelled fishy, and I didn't mean seaweed or anchovies.

'Every table is booked tomorrow night, remember,' Gaela said.

'How about the table in the kitchen?'

She gazed at me, considering. 'It'll be hot in there with the oven on full blast,' she warned.

I could make a simple potion of elderberry flowers, frog spawn and adder's tongue to protect me from too much heat. But it was almost Midsummer's Eve. Pizza was the last thing I should be thinking about, much less a selkie with sea green-blue eyes.

'I'll be here at six o'clock,' I said.

CHAPTER 7

Puck wasn't in his official moonlit glade when I TAPed back to Fairyland in a mist of choc-malt milkshake. I found him in a glade near ancient Athens, chuckling with Fairy Pineapple, who was in charge of keeping pineapple spikes sharp. My mind strayed to pizza. What would pineapple be like as a topping? It was sweet like tomato and caramelised nicely when cooked ... but no one would go for pineapple on pizza ...

'And then I made myself into the shape of a stool, and she sat on me,' Puck was telling Fairy Pineapple. 'There she was, this wise old aunt, telling the family how her husband had died. Just as everyone was getting out their handkerchiefs, I slipped from under her bum and she fell sprawling on the floor, coughing and crying.'

I sighed. I'd heard this story a thousand times since I was a kid, plus the one about pretending to be some traveller's horse.

'Well, they had to laugh, didn't they?' said Puck, giggling at his own joke.

'Most humorous,' said Fairy Pineapple, hauling himself to his feet. He'd put on weight in the last millennium — an occupational hazard of having to eat pineapple sundaes every day to make sure the sharpness of the spices didn't affect the sweetness of the pineapple. Or so he said.

'Hilarious,' I said. 'Look, we need to discuss the timing of our Midsummer's Eve revels now the humans have arranged this play. We don't want them to be an anticlimax. How about —'

I stopped as I saw Oberon stride into the glade.

'Shh, here comes His Majesty,' whispered Puck, noticing him at the same time.

'And here my mistress,' muttered Fairy Pineapple. 'Would that he were gone!' He tried to hide his bulk behind an olive tree.

I flew up into the tree's branches to hide a moment before Titania marched in, followed by Moth and Cobweb. The last thing I needed right now was to spend an hour giving Her Majesty a foot rub.

Titania stopped and glared at her husband. She was wearing a new dress of silvered moonlight, with dew-drop diamonds in her hair.

Oberon gave her a condescending look back. 'Ill met by moonlight, proud Titania,' he sneered.

I sighed. I'd hoped they would have made up their quarrel in time for the revels.

'What, jealous Oberon?' Titania declaimed, in true royal fashion. 'Fairies, skip hence. I have forsworn his bed and company.'

She turned to leave, but Oberon grabbed her arm. 'Tarry, rash wanton. Am not I your lord?'

Titania pulled away. 'Then I must be your lady,' she spat at him, 'but I know when you crept away from Fairyland, pretending to be "Corin", to recite love poems to amorous Phillida.'

They were at it then, like a pair of battling unicorns, flinging declamations back and forth.

Cobweb looked embarrassed. Moth stared at a beetle slowly beetling its way through the glade, as if he was able to turn off his ears and not listen to their quarrel. Being Moth and able to focus on only one thing at a time, he probably could.

I hoped Their Majesties wouldn't get carried away

again. Last time he was in a rage Oberon had turned every jar of Dew Brew blue for three days; and Titania had made all of earth's roses black with white skulls on them till she calmed down and ordered her courtiers to fix the problem. It had taken us days to paint the roses back to their proper colours, and weeks to change the memories of the humans who'd noticed them. It was clear we'd missed a few, because the design began to appear on pirate flags, and later on bikies' biceps.

'How long do you intend to stay within this wood?' demanded Oberon.

'Till after Theseus's wedding day,' Titania replied.

Oh, great. If Her Majesty planned to stay here until the Midsummer's Eve revels, we'd need to organise more attendants than she needed in the well-planned tidiness of Fairyland.

Titania stared at her husband in challenge. 'Dance with me by moonlight then. Or if not, shun me, and I will spare your haunts.'

'Give me that boy,' said Oberon flatly, 'and I will dance with you.'

'Not for your fairy kingdom. Fairies, away!' Titania vanished. A second later Cobweb disappeared too.

Moth looked up from the beetle and blinked.

'They went that way,' I hissed.

'Thanks, Peaseblossom,' he said, and vanished after them.

I should fade away as well, I thought, and get back to the paperwork. But there was something in Oberon's face that stopped me. I stared down at him. What was he planning?

'Puck?' said Oberon thoughtfully with a strange smile. 'Come here.'

'Yes, Your Majesty?' Puck's tone declared that he hadn't heard a word of the highly personal quarrel.

'You know the flower that with just a drop in someone's eyes makes them fall madly in love with the next creature they see?'

'Of course, sire. Heartsease, or love-in-idleness.'

'Fetch me some,' ordered His Majesty. 'Now!'

Why did Oberon want the flower for himself? Why not just get Puck to apply it?

Puck bowed. 'I'll put a girdle round about the earth in forty minutes,' he promised, and vanished in a small puff of chocolate-covered coffee beans.

Forty minutes! Puck was getting old. It would have taken me forty milliseconds. High time I took over his job.

Suddenly Oberon shimmered into invisibility. I did the same, up in the olive tree branches. A second later Demetrius strode into the glade with Helena running after him.

Demetrius stopped and turned on her. 'I love you not, therefore pursue me not.'

Mr Magnificent was still his charming self, it seemed.

'Where are Lysander and fair Hermia?' he demanded.

Helena opened her mouth, but Demetrius didn't give her time to answer him.

'The one I'll stop, the other stops me,' he declared, still glaring at Helena.

I tried to work out what he meant. Was he speaking literally or metaphorically, or both? Was he really going to kill Lysander? Was Hermia going to kill him? It would be hard to blame her, even though we fairies didn't go in for killing much. Why bother when enchantments were so much more fun? I suspected Demetrius just meant that he was dying of love for Hermia. Although more likely it was indigestion from too much baklava at lunch.

Demetrius put his hands on his hips. 'You told me they were sneaking into this wood; and here am I ...'

Helena looked at him pleadingly. She'd put flowers in her hair, but they'd wilted and made her look like a walking compost bin.

'They will be here,' she said, still out of breath from running. 'I heard them planning it. Demetrius, please —'

'Get yourself gone,' he snarled. 'And follow me no more.'

He pushed her away. I hoped she'd kick him in the shins and then march back to Athens. But of course she didn't. She just stood there looking at him, a hurt expression on her face.

'Do I entice you?' he demanded. 'Do I speak you fair? Or, rather, do I not in plainest truth tell you, I do not, nor I cannot love you?'

Helena shook her head. 'Even for that I love you more. I am your spaniel,' she added in a little-girl voice that set my teeth on edge. 'Only give me leave, unworthy as I am, to follow you.'

A bit of drama at the Midsummer's Eve revels was excellent, but these two left a sour taste.

Demetrius gave Helena one last angry look. 'I will not stay for your questions. Let me go. Or, if you follow me, believe me when I say I'll do you mischief in the wood.'

He ran off into the trees, obviously still intent on one thing — finding Hermia and Lysander. I began to think he might really be planning to kill Lysander.

Helena watched him go. 'I'll follow you and make a heaven of hell, to die upon the hand I love so well,' she whispered. She lifted her skirts — heavy with prickles by now — and ran after him.

Helena was a ninny and Demetrius was a bully. It was true that Lysander shouldn't have been courting Hermia without her father's consent. But he did love her, and she loved him. I couldn't let Demetrius kill Lysander, especially not so near Midsummer's Eve.

I was just about to follow the two foolish humans when Puck TAPed back into the glade, his hands full of heartsease flowers.

The air shivered with moonbeams and the scent of ginger chocolate fudge as Oberon popped back into visibility. He looked thoughtful.

'Have you the flower there?' he asked Puck. 'I pray you, give it to me.'

Puck handed him the pile of flowers, carefully not asking what His Majesty intended to do with them, but just as obviously waiting in case he should feel like explaining.

Oberon smiled. I shivered. I'd seen a smile like that on a snake about to eat a frog. I loved Their Majesties, of course. They would not be King and Queen if they didn't have the power to make us all adore them. But I didn't like them much.

'I know a bank where the wild thyme blows,' said Oberon softly. 'Where oxlips and the nodding violet grows, quite over-canopied with luscious woodbine, with sweet musk-roses and with eglantine: there sleeps Titania sometime of the night … and with the juice of this I'll streak her eyes, and make her full of hateful fantasies.'

'Oh, excellent plan, Your Majesty,' said Puck loyally.

Was this what unenchanted love was? I thought, gazing at Oberon so gleefully plotting against his wife. What fantasies was he about to arrange for Titania using the love potion in his hands? He intended her to fall desperately in love with the first person or beast she saw upon waking. Who did he have in mind?

Oberon grinned and handed Puck back some of the flowers. 'You'll also find a disdainful youth running through the wood with a maiden running after him. Drip some of this into his eyes so that as soon as he sees her he loves her far more than she loves him. Meet me back here at cock crow.'

'Fear not, my lord, your servant shall do so,' said Puck.

I blinked in amazement. Oberon was actually going to help a bunch of humans? I'd underestimated him. Once Demetrius had the drops in his eyes, he'd love Helena and give up chasing Hermia and Lysander. They would be safe with Lysander's aunt, and old Egeus might even forgive them once Demetrius had married Helena. As for Demetrius and Helena, they deserved each other.

PING! A summons from Titania.

I sighed and vanished into a cloud of cocoa with marshmallows.

Her Majesty was still in the Athenian wood, just as she had told Oberon, and planned to stay there till she'd enjoyed Theseus and Hippolyta's wedding, and mine to Flossie, and all the other Midsummer's Eve revels. She'd settled herself in a fairly pretty glade with olive trees and the same moon that we had in Fairyland, but only one of them.

Moth and Cobweb were in the glade with her. Cobweb raised an eyebrow at me. I winked back. Moth just fluttered in midair, waiting for someone to give him an order. He was good at that.

I gazed around. An Athenian grove was no place for a Fairy Queen to spend her day, much less to sleep. Too many prickles, hedgehogs and imperfect wildflowers, not to mention owls hunting mice once the sun went down. Also spiders — the venomous kind, not the jewelled-cobweb kind — and maybe even the odd adder. But there was nothing I could do about it till Titania realised the place needed some work to bring it up to royal standards.

'Come now,' she ordered. 'A roundel and a fairy song.'

I sighed. *This* was why we needed Elvis in Fairyland. We fairies were good at many things — turning milk sour, travelling to Alpha Centauri in forty seconds (don't bother trying it — the weather there is terrible), and, okay, we did dance divinely. Wings helped when you needed to be light-footed. But our music sucked.

Cobweb held out his hand. I took it, then nudged Moth.

'Which dance are we doing?' he asked.

I sighed again. We only had four dances. One was for the Midsummer's Eve revels; one was a rain dance. The third needed at least forty fairies and two full moons.

'Number four,' I said patiently.

'Oh, good, I like that one.' Moth took my hand.

Cobweb hummed the tune — not hard as it had only five notes — and we danced, our wings flickering, our tiptoes lightly touching the Athenian soil.

Titania watched us for forty-three seconds, then grew bored. She clapped her hands. 'Enough! Now, you have a third of a minute to kill cankers in the musk-rosebuds, and to go to war with the bats and take their leather wings.'

I sighed a third time, then tried to make it look like a yawn. Their Majesties hated anything flying above them, but it was a bit hard on the bats to remove their wings. What was a wingless bat to do?

Titania was still giving orders. 'And hush the clamorous owl that nightly hoots and wonders at our quaint spirits.'

In other words, tidy the place up and make it look like Fairyland.

The three of us fluttered around the glade, picking up prickles and the odd snake, a few caterpillars and a confused hedgehog looking for beetles.

I found the bats hanging upside down in a tree hollow.

'Quick,' I hissed. 'Out! Titania's on the war path.'

The biggest bat opened its eyes and stared at me, then recognised my wings. 'Thanks, mate,' it said.

The bats waited till Her Majesty's back was turned, then flapped quietly out of the glade and away.

I looked at the owl sitting in the branches above. 'As for you, keep your beak shut till Her Majesty has gone.'

The owl nodded silently.

Meanwhile, Moth and Cobweb had arranged a new grassy bank soft with moss and dotted with tender-petalled flowers that didn't grow in Greece at this time. They were going to play havoc with the Greek ecosystem. I'd seen Greece a thousand years in the future and there were wildflowers everywhere. This must have been where they began.

At last Titania nodded, satisfied. She lay on the mossy bank to test it for softness, gestured to Moth to shove the pillow moss a bit higher, then ordered, 'Sing me now asleep.' Sleep was the best way to escape fairy singing. I was just about to gesture for us all to begin when she added, 'Then to your offices and let me rest.'

Oops. Leaving her all alone wasn't a good idea. If Cobweb and I stayed to guard her, or even Moth, she couldn't get into too much trouble when Oberon put the love potion in her eyes. I hesitated. Should I warn her of Oberon's plan?

But if I did that, Oberon would find out I'd eavesdropped. Titania would know that I'd eavesdropped too. A fairy who eavesdropped on the King might eavesdrop on the Queen. To say she'd be displeased was an understatement. There'd be no promotion to Puck's permanent assistant in Oberon's court. Nor would the Queen be grateful to me. Fairy Queens didn't believe in the 'don't shoot the messenger' principle. If I blurted out her marriage troubles in front of the others, I'd be raking unicorn dung for at least a century.

Pretending ignorance was best, I told myself. After all, what trouble could she get into here, even with the love potion in her eyes? The bats were gone, the owl was safely out of sight high in a tree. We'd even removed the hedgehog.

The three of us arranged ourselves ready to sing, bass to baritone to tenor. I was a tenor and didn't have a bad voice either. You didn't get far at the Fairy Court if you didn't sing and dance, no matter how bad the song or music.

'One, two, three,' I commanded softly, and we began our song:

'You spotted snakes with double tongue,

Thorny hedgehogs, be not seen;

Newts and blind-worms, do no wrong,

Come not near our Fairy Queen.'

See what I mean? We wouldn't even make it into the audience at a talent quest.

'Philomel, with melody

Sing in our sweet lullaby;

Lulla, lulla, lullaby, lulla, lulla, lullaby.'

Titania's eyes closed.

'*Never harm,*' we sang, more softly now, except for Moth, who was attempting a descant. I nudged him, and he lowered his voice but not his pitch.

'*Nor spell nor charm,*

Come our lovely lady nigh;

So, good night, with lullaby.

Weaving spiders, come not here;

Hence, you long-legg'd spinners, hence!

Beetles black, approach not near;

Worm nor snail, do no offence.'

Was the Queen asleep? I gestured to the others for one more verse.

'*Philomel, with melody*

Sing in our sweet lullaby;

Lulla, lulla, lullaby, lulla, lulla, lullaby.'

I held up my hand for silence, and nudged Moth when he opened his mouth again. The Queen was deeply asleep now. The day's tantrums must have tired her out.

She looked beautiful lying there in her green silk dress that matched the moss, except where it was trimmed with gold. Her hair hung in long blonde tresses down the bank. Even her snores were deliciously alluring. And sometime soon, Oberon was going to squeeze heartsease juice in her eyes so she would fall in love with ... Who? Or what?

I looked around carefully, but nothing had entered the grove, not even a beetle. The only things here that Titania could fall in love with were the wildflowers, which should be safe enough. Actually, a Fairy Queen in love with a rose or asphodel or anemone might be peaceful.

As long as she didn't fall in love with me, I thought. Even raking out unicorn dung wouldn't be punishment enough if that happened. I needed to get well away from ancient Athens and this glade until Her Majesty was safely in love with whatever she first saw when she woke.

After all, she had told us to leave her once she fell asleep. Plus I had a table booked at the Leaning Tower of Pizza for 6 pm.

The Athenian glade vanished into a fog of after-dinner mints.

CHAPTER 8

Their choc-mint scent was still with me when I appeared on the footpath outside the pizza shop. I blinked. No long line of customers — Gaela must have told them she wasn't opening tonight. But there were other changes too. The cats had vanished. The café's windows gleamed. Someone had painted its sign in gold. Even the pavement seemed scrubbed.

I opened the door.

'Do you have a reservation, sir? I'm afraid we're booked out tonight.'

I stared. The door attendant was tall, dark and handsome, with pale lips and brilliant white fangs. Not Guyye, but close enough in looks to be his sister. I wondered suddenly if the Fairy Floss ever collected vampire fangs. I wasn't sure I'd want any hanging in our trophy room. But I supposed they'd crumble to dust with daylight.

'Yes,' I told her firmly. 'Name of Pete for 6 pm.'

The attendant looked at the book on the counter. The newly painted counter, with a vase of stylishly arranged branches painted black and silver.

'Ah, yes, Mr Pete. Your table is in the kitchen, sir.' She made it sound as if the kitchen was the best place for me, preferably lined up on the 'to be sucked for supper' bench. She looked disdainfully at my hoodie. 'May I take your, ahem, jacket, sir?'

'No, thank you,' I said. This was not the time to display my fairy wings.

I gazed around. Half the café tables — each with a fresh white tablecloth and black twig decorations in a crystal vase — were still empty. The customers at the others looked different from last night's: men in suits that must have cost the food bill for an entire village; women wearing clinging dresses and with smooth faces like transplanted baby cheeks — all of them exuding enough glamour to power a small city.

The vampires sitting with them hadn't even bothered to dress for the occasion. When you had as much charisma as a vampire, you could wear an old raincoat and everyone would remember you as elegant. The vampires here tonight had stuck with Vampire Classic: black trousers and black turtlenecks for both the men and the women. Only their hands were bright: loaded with rings ranging from antique to pop art, decorated with gold, rubies and diamonds — proof of the riches they'd looted from their victims for centuries.

It was hard to recognise the café as the same place I'd been in last night. Even the floor was polished, though not enough to show the reflections the vampires didn't have. Only the scent was familiar: pizza crust and melted cheese and the faint tang of seaweed.

A young man entered the café behind me and approached the reception desk. 'Excuse me, I wonder if —'

The attendant cut him off. 'Do you have a reservation, sir? I'm afraid we're booked out tonight.'

'No, I just hoped there might be time for a quick vegetarian pizza before the people who made the reservation arrive?' He spoke as if he could already taste the artichoke hearts, cheese, grilled capsicum, marinated eggplant, mushroom and Gaela's special tomato sauce. It was the voice of a true pizza lover, lured here by the menu, not by magic.

'Scram,' said the attendant softly. The glamour about her changed as the beast within erupted. I could smell ancient blood …

The door banged shut. Footsteps sounded out on the footpath, then stopped. I hoped the young man had just hopped onto his bicycle or into his car, not been gathered up for a vampire supper. Then again, all of Guyye's … friends? family? colleagues? were probably already in here.

'Pete!' Gaela looked up from talking to one of the suited men at a table with Guyye. She seemed truly glad to see me. 'Come into the kitchen.'

I caught snippets of some intense conversations as we passed between the tables.

'… that land is three metres underwater after every big storm. We couldn't possibly change the zoning laws.'

'Of course you can,' replied a vampire voice smoothly, dripping glamour. 'There's room for six hundred houses and a supermarket there.'

'Yes … yes, of course I can,' the first speaker said, sounding dazed. She took a bite of pizza (House Special with anchovies). 'The owner of this café … you're a friend of hers?'

'A very good friend.' Just a hint of fang accompanied the answer.

The first speaker looked reassured.

Vampire glamour was irresistible, but it wasn't love. The vampires needed Gaela too, needed the warmth and security of her café, the love Gaela gave to her pizzas, and the love humans feel for selkies too.

'What do you call a group of vampires?' I asked Gaela as we walked towards the kitchen.

She looked around nervously in case anyone had heard, then grabbed my hand and ushered me through the swinging doors. As usual, all the topping ingredients were laid out neatly on the stainless-steel benches, and the dough was rising in small mounds ready to be stretched flat. The giant oven, with its small door and the long spade to slide the pizzas in and out, was already hot. The room smelled of herbed tomato sauce and no glamour whatsoever.

'Okay, what do you call a group of vampires?' she demanded.

'A bunch of suckers. But it's their companions who are the suckers, right?'

'Pete —' But Gaela broke off as Guyye came in. The worry left her face at once. 'Yes, Guyye, darling?'

'Table three would like a salad. Senator Grunk is on a diet.'

'But we don't offer —'

'Of course we offer salads, don't we, Gaela, darling? Senator Grunk is chair of the acquisitions committee. Big decisions will be made here tonight.'

'Yes, of course we offer salads,' repeated Gaela obediently. She blinked at the ingredients on the bench. 'There's artichoke hearts and olives and grilled capsicum and tomatoes ...'

'I'll run out and get some lettuce,' I offered.

'Good boy,' said Guyye, not quite patting me on the head. He vanished into the main room again.

Gaela stared after him, still vague and adoring, so I didn't bother going outside to TAP back a few years to when this place had been a deli. I bought two Greek salads, a tub of tabouli, and an Aussie special with lettuce, beetroot, tomato, sliced orange and a halved hard-boiled egg. I had the salads set out on the kitchen bench by the time Gaela came out of her glamour.

She blinked at me, then at the salads, then began arranging parts of each on a new plate without asking questions.

'To table three?' I asked, picking up the plate.

'You're a customer, not a waiter,' she protested.

'I'm a friend.'

She looked at me, surprised, then nodded. I made my way out to table three.

'Just a small change to the labour laws,' a vampire was saying to a woman in a tight-fitting dress, 'would mean that no one needs to pay workers unless they *ask* to be paid. And ten-year-olds are quite capable of running call centres, which would be an education all of its own, so no need for schools. That would be an enormous budgetary saving ...'

'Do bring your colleagues tomorrow night,' Guyye was saying to the business types sitting either side of him.

I slid the salad onto the table just as Senator Grunk agreed that there was no need to call for tenders for the operation of the new Blood Bank, and, yes, she could have a contract for a Blood Bank manager drawn up by Wednesday night.

Guyye grabbed my arm as I turned back to the kitchen. 'Get Gaela out here with the next order,' he hissed. 'Fast.'

The best pizza in the world had lured these people here. And vampire glamour was conning them into staying. But already some of the non-vampire faces were puzzled, as if wondering exactly what they had agreed to. They needed a hit of Gaela and her selkie magic, and then they would be happy again, I thought, which was why Guyye had ordered me to fetch her.

Just then she came out anyway, a Three Cheese and Two Mushroom in one hand and a Haloumi and Potato (gluten-free) in the other. The room glowed with reassurance again.

Love is a many-splendoured thing, I thought. And now Guyye has found a way to make it profitable as well.

I pushed through the doors into the kitchen and sat at the tiny table next to the oven.

'Guyye doesn't want me as a waiter,' I told Gaela when she came in again. 'I'd better act like a customer.'

Her eyes sparkled as she nodded. Guyye must have done his wrist-kissing routine again. The glow faded just a little as she asked, 'What kind of pizza would you like tonight?'

I pretended to consult the menu. 'Garlic and tomato. Hold the anchovies.'

She really did look at me then. 'No garlic tonight.'

'Not even in the tomato sauce?'

'Never in the tomato sauce. Never has been.'

I stood up. 'Then maybe I'd better find another pizza shop that serves garlic.'

'Maybe you should!'

'Gaela ...' I reached for her hand.

She pulled it back, then slowly reached towards me. I wasn't sure what would have happened next if Guyye hadn't pushed through the kitchen doors.

'Table eight wants a steak,' he told Gaela.

'A stake? Excellent idea,' I said.

He looked at me as if I were a slug, then smiled at Gaela. The room filled with moonbeams as she smiled back.

I didn't know where she was going to get a steak from. And just then I didn't care. I vanished.

I didn't go far. There was a seat on the boardwalk about fifty metres from the café door. The air I displaced when I landed next to it only had a tinge of white chocolate fudge.

I'd just got settled when the banshees strolled by hand in hand — or fuzz in fuzz. Banshees were the colour of night — every night and every kind of darkness — so I didn't notice them till they were right in front of me.

'Sorry, the Leaning Tower of Pizza isn't open tonight,' I said.

The female banshee shook her head. I knew she was female because she had longer hair ... or whatever that droopy, wavy stuff was. (That bit of knowledge probably isn't any use to you, because if a mortal sees a banshee it means they're about to die.)

She pointed to the café. 'Lights on. Smells good!'

'It's only open for special customers tonight,' I said.

I didn't add that the Leaning Tower of Pizza would probably never have its midnight sitting again. Vampires had no need to enchant banshees, bunyips, trolls or ogres as they tended not to be elected as politicians or the head of the real-estate zoning board or directors of multinational corporations.

'We special,' said the taller banshee, his darkness mingling just a little more with his partner's.

I smiled at them. I couldn't help it. Love swam around them like tadpoles in a pond.

'Yes,' I said, 'you're special.' True love, freely chosen love: there was nothing more special in the world. Not that I wanted freely chosen love, I reminded myself, not with all its bickering and jealousy. 'But your way of being special won't get you pizza here tonight.'

'You sad,' said the female banshee.

I thrust away the image of Gaela's sea-coloured eyes. 'I won't get a pizza tonight either. And I really like pizza.'

They both looked at me with their eyes that were darker than dark except for the faintest glint among their swirls.

'That not why,' said the female. 'You in love.'

I shook my head. 'Selkie enchantment doesn't work on fairies. I really am a fairy,' I added quickly. 'My wings are under my hoodie.'

The two lengths of darkness both shrugged.

'Banshee know human from fairy,' said the male. 'You not in selkie love. You in real love.'

I shook my head. Banshees specialised in forecasting death, not diagnosing love. And I'd been playing around with love potions since I first learned to fly.

'Not possible. Only fairy royalty fall in love freely. I've never even heard of an ordinary fairy who fell in love before the potion was placed in their eyes. But Gaela is my friend. I care about her.'

The darknesses looked at me thoughtfully. They had almost blended into one now. 'We care about her too,' they said. 'How we help?'

'I'm trying to figure it out.'

I was also trying to figure out if Gaela needed my help. After all, she knew her love for Guyye was probably just glamour and she'd still chosen to make pizza for his guests. She *needed* my help, I decided, but she didn't *want* it.

'We think how we help too,' said the darknesses, then they vanished into the gloom.

I stayed on the bench, hoping to work out what to do. Gaela was my friend. Nothing more than that. But you didn't let down your friends.

Far out at sea I thought I saw a flash that might be a sea serpent hoping for some pizza. But the sea serpent was out of luck tonight too. And probably forever.

I gazed at the white-frilled waves a while longer. If I could prove to Gaela that Guyye didn't love her but was only using her, then maybe ... Maybe what? Gaela was *happy* with Guyye, whatever his motives. And that was what mattered, wasn't it? People being neatly enchanted into happiness.

Look at Titania and Oberon, bickering away the millennia because they'd never had heartsease potion put into their eyes. They could have used the potion and been happy for eternity, but had chosen not to be enchanted into loving each other. Why? Why choose to experience unhappiness when you didn't have to? Why did people want to choose their own job, or what clothes they wore, or who they could marry? Why not let your King or Queen choose for you, as we fairies did?

Yet Gaela had chosen pizza over her selkie friends and family. Maybe she would still want Guyye if she knew he didn't love her; knew he didn't like her pizzas, just the opportunities they gave him. But she had a right to know the truth. She had a right to choose.

And whatever she chose, I decided, I'd support her, even if she chose to live with Guyye and his mob forever.

CHAPTER 9

The vampires, all except Guyye, sauntered out a few minutes afterwards, moving like buttered velvet. No one did elegant saunter like a vampire. They clustered by the lamp post, then *zing*! A cloud of bats flapped away.

Guyye came out next. I hadn't expected he'd stay to help with the washing-up. He paused at the door and blew a kiss towards the kitchen.

'See you tomorrow night, sweet cheeks,' he called.

Zing!

But this time a bee followed the bat.

I didn't have to fly far. The vampires were living in a classy-looking apartment building six blocks away from the pizza shop. You know the kind: fifty matching shrubs tortured into square blocks out the front, and a million windows like a movie star's sunglasses. The vampires had the penthouse, but this penthouse was underground.

I buzzed through the door behind Guyye, then perched on a light fitting on the high ceiling as he *zinged* back into human shape.

The other vampires were lounging on black steel lounges. They'd changed into an assortment of clothes from thousands of years of fashion — I supposed they chose their favourite outfit from whatever era they'd lived in before they became vampires. There was a Roman toga; what looked like the dress Cleopatra wore to seduce Mark Antony; Queen Elizabeth I's coronation gown; John Wayne's jeans and cowboy hat.

Guyye wore an ancient Hittite's tunic of embroidered leather, with enough gold necklaces and armlets to sink a cruise ship. He pulled the iron door shut and bolted it. Didn't bother me. I couldn't go through a locked door, but I could go backwards or forwards in time till the door wasn't there.

I settled myself on a comfortable twist of steel not too close to the light bulb as Guyye flung himself into an armchair.

'Humanity is wearing,' he said, yawning. His fangs gleamed in the light. 'Such petty, boring little lives. But a year of deals like tonight and we'll be set up for another millennia.'

A female with a ring on her delicate white finger that I recognised from Julius Caesar's time held up a crystal glass. I didn't think the red stuff in it was wine.

'Want a snack, Guyye?' she offered. 'Pure virgin.'

'He's already eaten with his little lady love,' said another of the females snarkily.

Guyye grinned and gave a dramatic shiver. 'Me, snack on fish bait? Never.'

'Doesn't she expect a bit of vampirising?' asked the first female curiously.

Guyye laughed. His other teeth were yellow, I noticed, only the fangs were white and bright. I wondered how old he really was.

'She thinks I "respect" her,' he said. 'Pass me the flagon.'

He poured himself a glass of the red fluid. Yes, it was far too thick to be wine, or even raspberry cordial.

'Drink up before it congeals,' said the female with the ring. 'I want to go out hunting before daylight. Get rid of the stink of pizza.'

'But the plans,' said Guyye.

'They'll wait till tomorrow night, won't they, pretty boy?'

She moved towards him and they shared the kind of kiss I bet he'd never given Gaela.

Suddenly the room was full of bats again, then they were all gone. I didn't imagine they'd be back till nearly dawn.

I sat there on my light fitting, thinking. What if I could project that scene for Gaela so she could see Guyye kissing the other vampire? She'd learn that not only did he not love her, but he didn't even like her or respect her. He didn't even enjoy pizza.

Could I do it? I'd flicked up images for Queen Titania a thousand times, but that was in Fairyland with the power of her court around me. Could I do it by myself?

Suddenly I knew: whatever power I had, I'd use it to help Gaela. I could do this.

What would happen if Guyye turned up in the middle of us watching a scene from the past? He might convince Gaela I was playing a trick. She'd believe him too. She loved him. As long as Guyye was there, she'd never believe me.

And even if I did convince her, what then? Guyye would still turn up tomorrow night and she'd be under his glamour again, even if she didn't want to be.

I had to stop the vampires altogether. But how?

I also needed time to think.

I smiled. That, at least, I knew how to do.

In a true manipulation of time and place, I swiftly TAPed forward in time to the Moon, followed by a great storm of choc cherries scent. So much for Guyye's iron door, I thought smugly. By this future time, humans had created a couple of settlements on the Moon, but there were still plenty of empty-space craters where I could perch, return to my own shape and size, and simply think. Moon dust rose around me as I sat myself down, then settled slowly. I kept my wings still so I didn't dislodge any more.

What were my choices? Could I use a potion to ruin the vampires' plan? Fairy magic didn't work on vampires, but not all potions were magic. Non-magic potions still needed to be eaten or drunk though, which ruled them out. The only way to get a vampire to drink enough of such a potion would be to force the vampire's victim to take it before the vampire sucked their blood, and that would make me worse than a vampire.

Perhaps I could rub itching powder on their skin? I grinned. That would be fun. No way could they corrupt a pizza shop full of important patrons if they were scratching every ten seconds. Even vampire glamour couldn't cover that. Itching powder was easy to make too. You just needed to pick a giant stinging nettle, let it dry in the sun for six months or so — I could TAP that easily — then grind it into a powder while wearing protective clothing. (You did *not* want to breathe in that stuff!) And dust it over the naked vampires ...

But did vampires ever get naked? They seemed to change their clothes as easily as their shape. And everyone knew that female vampires slept in long white nightdresses and males in nineteenth-century evening clothes. I'd never get a chance to dust them with the itching powder. I bet they didn't have to hang their clothes in wardrobes either, so I couldn't even contaminate the fabric instead.

What other options were there? An armed attack? Fairies were safe from vampires, but how much damage could a fairy do to a vampire, even if it was in bat form? I could make myself a hundred feet tall, TAP back to ancient Athens and borrow King Theseus's sword, but as soon as I raised it, Guyye would only need to *zing* into bat shape and fly away.

No magic then. No violence either, which I was glad of as I'd never actually attacked anyone in my life. I even removed the ants from Her Majesty's path with care and dignity.

Which left ... I grinned.

Garlic.

I TAPed back to the vampires' penthouse. It would be sunrise in an hour, and I didn't think they'd want to cut their return too fine and risk crumbling to dust in the first ray of light.

The first one back was the vampire Guyye had kissed. Her lips were even redder now, and wore a smile of deep satisfaction. I watched as she *zinged* into a white nightdress, then went through another door. That must be where they kept their coffins.

Guyye was next, looking well-fed and smug. He also looked far too handsome when he'd changed into evening dress and headed for his coffin.

I waited till the last vampire had returned, bolted the door, yawned and headed off for a nice safe sleep. And so they were safe in their underground luxury penthouse with a securely bolted door and no windows. Sort of.

I TAPed to the nearest supermarket and filled my trolley with all the garlic in the place. The other customers looked at me a bit oddly, as did those in the next fourteen supermarkets I visited. But at last I had enough garlic.

Okay, focus time. I TAPed each trolley-load of garlic back to the vampires' living room one by one. The place was a metre deep in garlic cloves when I'd finished.

I stood in the middle of the garlicky room and grinned. Garlic wouldn't kill a vampire — only a wooden stake in the heart did that, or sunlight — but it would make them nauseous and weak. Not a single vampire would be able to walk through this room to open the iron door. And there were no other exits from the apartment. No windows underground. They were trapped by the very measures that made them safe.

I knew it wouldn't be forever. Vampires were strong — as long as they stayed away from garlic. They could burrow out of their coffin room, but it might take them a week to do it.

Even if it only took a single night for them to escape, it was enough time for me to show Gaela my recording and give her a free choice. Did she want to live in an enchanted happiness forever?

I bit my lip, wondering what she would choose.

CHAPTER 10

Time to return to the Leaning Tower of Pizza, before Gaela went to sleep. I TAPed back two hundred years before the apartment had been built, to get past the locked door, then TAPed two hundred years forward again.

I flew slowly towards the café. An owl hooted at me, annoyed that I'd invaded his evening patrol; and a few possums eyed me warily.

The cats were back on the pizza shop's windowsills. They gave me identical looks of disgust as though to say, 'Your kind never brings fish bits.'

I landed on the footpath, changed to human size and quickly pulled my hoodie over my wings. Was I doing the right thing?

And even if it was right, would Gaela forgive me?

I took a deep breath, inhaling the scent of hot pizza crust and anchovies, and opened the door.

Gaela was sitting at the kitchen table, drawing patterns with her finger on the tomato sauce-stained cloth. From here the sauce looked like blood. Her face was as blank as a concrete wall. She didn't even look up as I walked in.

I shivered: she'd let the oven go out and the dawn breeze was cool. I shut the door, then pulled up a chair next to her. This was going to be hard.

'Gaela ...'

'That's my name,' she agreed.

'I followed Guyye after he left here tonight. I ... I'm sorry, but I was worried for you.' I gulped at the hard blank look on her face. 'He and his friends were talking —'

'About using my magic to enchant real-estate developers, public servants, politicians — whoever they want to influence to get power or money, or just for the fun of playing with humans. I'm not a fool, Pete,' she added flatly.

I looked at her then. Really looked at her. Her selkie enchantment had never touched me, but I'd still seen her beauty, her joy in making pizzas and being in the sea. Now I saw far more. I saw courage. Gaela still loved Guyye. How could she help it when he'd used his glamour on her? But she hadn't let that stop her from seeing what was happening around her. Even now, she fought against the glamour. And she'd won.

'No,' I said softly. 'You're not a fool.'

'Guyye doesn't even like pizza.' A tear crept down her cheek. Suddenly her face looked like it might crumple. 'I ... I just wanted to believe he did. He doesn't love me either. I watched those two banshees last night — their whole world was each other. And even when that first kind of love fades, an even stronger, deeper love will still be there.' She took a breath, then said, 'I don't love Guyye. I've realised that too. If he walked in right now, I'd feel his enchantment again — I wouldn't be able to help it. But enchantment isn't love.'

'But enchantment can make you love,' I said. 'I don't mean you should put up with Guyye,' I added quickly. 'You need to be rid of him forever. But love is ... love ... no matter whether it comes naturally or from magic.'

'I don't think it is,' she said quietly. 'I think love comes in a million flavours. Enchantment is one of those flavours, but not the one I want.'

I took her firm and slightly floury hand. 'What are you going to do?'

She shrugged, but her hand grasped mine as if it gave her comfort. 'The only thing I can do. Shut the café down today, before Guyye wakes up. And swim away.'

She looked longingly around the kitchen, at the giant pizza oven, at the shining stainless-steel benches, the neat bowls of ingredients, the mounds of rising dough.

'I ... I should have left already. I've just been trying to find the will and the energy to leave. Guyye won't find me underwater.' She gave a sad smile. 'He wouldn't even recognise me in seal shape. If I stay here, he'll keep using my selkie enchantment and pizza to attract people he wants to influence, even if I don't marry him.'

'But this café is your dream,' I said.

'Yes, just a dream. I'll go back to the sea where I belong.'

'But what about pizza?'

Her smile this time held a lifetime of regret. A long lifetime, for she and I were both immortal. 'Whoever heard of a selkie making pizza?'

'Whoever heard of a sea serpent eating pizza? Or a fairy or a pair of banshees? Look,' I took her hand again, then dropped it quickly because it felt too … too right, 'I've sort of tricked the vampires.'

She stared at me. 'What?'

'I filled their living room with garlic. It'll keep them away for at least a night, maybe longer. But you've got more time to escape Guyye than you thought. Swim away where he'll never find you and start again. You can open another pizza shop.'

'I … I don't know if I've got the courage to do that. Not again.' She drooped in her chair, like seaweed washed too far up the beach by the tide.

'Of course you can! You've seen through vampire glamour! You can do anything.'

She looked at me as if she hoped I would say something more, do something more. But what else could I say or do?

'Maybe,' she said at last. 'Or maybe I should just do what I was born to do — be a selkie.'

I tried frantically to think of a way to make it better. 'Perhaps you'll fall in love with one of those enchanted fishermen.'

Her sea-deep eyes met mine. 'But what if I fell out of love with him? I'd either vanish into the waves, or stay with him for his poor short human life pretending I wasn't bored. Selkies don't fall in love with humans forever,' she added softly. 'That's always been our tragedy. And theirs.'

'There's a flower,' I said slowly. 'Having its essence dropped in your eyes makes you love the first person you see afterwards for always. It's what Flossie and I will be given at our wedding. If you did find a fisherman, I could put the drops in your eyes. You'd love him his whole life then.'

'No.'

Suddenly it seemed desperately urgent that I make her understand. 'You're choosing to be lonely?'

Once again she looked at me for so long I felt uncomfortable. What was she waiting for me to say?

'I know what true love is now,' she said at last, her voice as quiet as the sea's ripples on the sand. 'Now I've seen it, I can't live with less.'

'You mean the banshees? Yes, that's true love. I don't think they'll ever bicker or play tricks on each other.'

Her expression was impossible to read. 'Yes, the banshees. I'll miss them.' She managed another smile, one of courage, wistfulness and determination but with a hint of anguish that made me want to cry. 'Maybe I'll find another selkie who wants to make pizza. Though I haven't met one in four hundred years.'

I pushed away the cold thought of Gaela with another selkie.

'But what if you love each other but make each other unhappy?' I asked. 'What if you get angry at each other? Or feel anguished if they get hurt? Even if you were to find a selkie who loves pizza, you could still let me put the potion in your eyes and your partner's too. Then you'll never know unhappiness, anguish or anger.'

She met my eyes. 'I choose it all. The unhappiness, the anger and the anguish.' Her voice took on a new strength. 'Maybe it's the certainty of eventual pain and loss that makes true love so deep. There has to be a price for something as profound as love. But thank you for the offer.'

'Really, it's no trouble.' Except it might be. An unlicensed enchantment could get me demoted to Third Assistant Firefly. 'It's what friends do for each other,' I added.

Gaela took my hand. 'And you are my friend.' She hesitated, then said, 'Because you're my friend — my only friend, my dearest friend — will you swim with me?'

I couldn't do it. If I went for a swim now, it would take at least an hour for my wings to dry. I had to get back in time for the Midsummer's Eve preparations, and I'd already spent so many hours here I'd have to slice time into micro-micro-microseconds to manage it. And what if the glow-worms had the sniffles? Or the fireflies were allergic to this year's vintage Dew Brew? Trust me, you didn't want sneezing fireflies lighting up your enchanted glade.

But no matter how long I lived, I would never get a chance to swim with Gaela again. Never follow her through the bright water. I knew this was goodbye, and I couldn't bear for it to end just yet.

I didn't hesitate; I kept hold of her hand and let her lead me through the back door.

When she shut it, I knew that she would never enter the Leaning Tower of Pizza again.

The sun sat like a tomato on the horizon, turning the sky pink around it. We walked down the sand to the froth bubbling at the edges of the waves. Gaela threw off the velvet dress she must have worn especially for Guyye's guests, and the shoes that must have pinched her webbed feet.

I pulled off my jeans and underpants and hoodie, and Gaela took my hand again as we walked into the water. Her hand was slightly webbed and cooler than a fairy or human hand.

I had felt water before. Fairies washed in babbling brooks; and I'd even been drenched by a few thunderstorms till I learned how to avoid them. But I had never felt water like this. The sea was alive and filled with living creatures. With Gaela's hand in mine, I could sense them all.

Waves nibbled my toes, then washed about my ankles. We walked until the water was waist high, then she pulled me under a wave and kept swimming, heading down.

There were rocks, and a long band of bright coral, and a thousand tiny fish that moved as one but with a thousand colours, while larger fish wandered among them.

The increasing sunlight filtered down through the water in a thousand tiny spears, turning the sand white or gold or green.

Gaela swam more strongly now, as if she was taking me somewhere. I didn't try to think where it might be, or why. I just let the water flow over my skin, and watched the sunbeams ripple and shiver all around us, and felt Gaela's hand holding mine, warm even though we were underwater, her body moving as if she was the waves themselves.

I had been a master of time since I was small, but I forgot time now. There was only the sea and Gaela and me.

Dimly I heard singing, far away but all around me too. No human voices sang like that, not even Elvis, and certainly not fairy instruments. I let the music wash around me. No words can describe the million songs the sea can sing to you when you swim with a selkie's hand holding yours.

At last we burst up through the surface. The sunlight embraced us, turning our skins to gold. All around there was only sea and sky and us.

Gaela held both my hands now as I trod water, my wings limp and useless behind me.

'Where are we?' I asked.

'The sea.'

She looked at me with those blue-green eyes, then leaned closer. Her lips tasted of waves and anchovies.

At last she pulled back and watched me silently as the sea crashed froth around our bodies.

Finally I knew what Gaela wanted me to say. I wanted to say it, I longed to say it, but I couldn't. I was a fairy and must do a fairy's duty. Gaela had a choice, but I didn't.

'What was that song?' I asked instead.

She nodded slightly, as if she'd realised at last that I could never say what she wanted to hear. 'That was whales singing. They call to each other across the ocean.'

'What did that song mean?'

'It was a kind of love song. It means welcome.'

'They were singing to you?'

'And you, maybe.'

I had to say it. 'I can't stay with you, Gaela. I have a job to do. And I'm getting married.' Neither explanation seemed enough, even to me. 'Fairies don't leave Fairyland,' I added. 'It isn't allowed.'

'You're here now.'

'I split a moment of time into an instant. If I stay too long, they'll notice. I … we have to go back.'

'Pete … that poet I rescued … I'll never forget the last line of his poem.'

I loved how my name sounded in her mouth. I never wanted to be called Peaseblossom again.

'What was it?' I managed to ask.

'The poem ends like this,' she said quietly.

'*Singing: "There dwells a loved one,*
But cruel is she,

She left lonely for ever

The kings of the sea."'

For a moment I couldn't speak. I saw her love now. She let me see it. It had all the beauty of waves rolling forever, from one ocean to another, never-ending like true love never ended. It held the song of the whales, the sea serpent, the tiny fish that flashed through the coral.

At last I said, 'I have to go back to the land.'

I feared ... hoped ... she'd refuse. Without her, I'd never make it to shore. And stuck here in the water with wet wings, I could never leave. But then I realised Gaela would never do that. That would trap me as much as an enchantment would.

Instead, she kissed me again. I tasted the salt of the waves, or her tears.

Or maybe they were my tears.

CHAPTER 11

Gaela didn't come out of the sea with me this time. As soon as I felt my feet touch sand, she let go of my hand and swam away, so fast I couldn't even make out her seal shape among the ripples.

I turned and walked up onto the sand dunes. I sat there, letting my wings dry, and thought about all kinds of things.

How if I'd used the love potion more often I could have prevented so many wars and arguments among humankind.

About Gaela's smile.

About how just a bit of magic could give humanity peace and plenty, and they'd never know they'd been enchanted.

About Gaela's tears, more salty than the sea.

The waves retreated with the tide, leaving seaweed draped on the sand, its scent reminding me of her. She was out there, somewhere. Free.

The wind whirled next to me and I smelled choc-chip muffins.

Moth appeared. 'Peaseblossom! Thank goodness!' he breathed. 'Ow!' he yelped as he trod on a bit of coral.

'What is it?' I asked, suddenly realising I'd forgotten to keep control of time since … I wasn't sure since when. But time had passed, here and in Fairyland too.

'Puck's drunk too much Dew Brew. Or he's going senile. It's all gone wrong! You have to come back.'

I reached into time and twisted it gently. 'Slow down. We'll get back the moment you came to find me. Tell me what's happened.'

Moth stopped hopping around and sat down beside me.

'Puck gave His Majesty the love potion,' he said breathlessly. 'The King squeezed some into Her Majesty's eyes as she lay sleeping, and told Puck to put some into Demetrius's eyes so he'd love Helena.'

'I know,' I interrupted. 'I saw His Majesty do it.'

'But Puck made a mistake and put the potion in Lysander's eyes instead,' wailed Moth. 'And now

Lysander's in love with Helena instead of Hermia. And then Puck gave the human actor called Bottom the head of a donkey, and Her Majesty woke up ...' He gulped. 'And fell in love with Bottom, donkey head and all. She's called us all to serve him. You too. Now! You have to fix it, Peaseblossom! Her Majesty's going to turn us all into slugs when she finds out!'

Suddenly all my doubts fell away. This was what I had been born for, trained for. There was a lot to put right, but I could do it — and when I had, I'd have Puck's job, or my name wasn't Peaseblossom. But the Queen's orders came first.

'Right, come on. Time to TAP,' I informed Moth.

'There's worse,' he said miserably, not moving.

I stared at him. 'What could be worse?'

'Oberon was pleased about the donkey head and Her Majesty looking,' he lowered his voice, 'er, foolish. But he was angry about Demetrius loving the wrong woman. So he called for more potion and now Demetrius loves Helena too, just like Lysander does.'

And Hermia, that good, loyal and determined girl, was now loved by no one, not even her father. She must be in anguish. This had to be put right.

I gathered up the strings of time and twisted them about Moth too. The scent of salt vanished. I smelled dark chocolate fudge with a hint of macadamia nuts.

Then we were in the Athenian glade again, about eight thousand years away from the Leaning Tower of Pizza, from any pizza, and from Gaela.

Time to get to work, and then live happily ever after.

I could hardly bear it.

The glade was just as I'd left it, except now, as well as Her Majesty, it held a large hairy weaver/actor with a donkey's head. The Queen of the Fairies looked as besotted as a two-year-old who's discovered ice cream.

Her arms were twisted about Bottom's thick donkey neck as she whispered into his furry ears, 'Thou art as wise as thou art beautiful.'

Bottom looked uneasy. I had a feeling he wasn't used to the most beautiful woman in the world throwing her arms around him. Or even any beautiful woman. Plus he must be feeling a bit woozy suddenly having only a donkey's brain to think with.

'Not so, neither,' he muttered. 'But if I had wit enough to get out of this wood, I have enough to serve mine own turn.'

I tried to work out what he meant. One thing was clear: he didn't want to be here, and he especially didn't want to be here with Titania.

Titania smiled seductively. 'Out of this wood do not desire to go,' she murmured, and there was magic in her voice now. 'You shall remain here, whether you will or no.'

Bottom tried to edge away. Titania wriggled onto his lap. He stopped, either because of her weight or her enchantment.

'I am a spirit of no common rate,' the Queen said, a tone of command in her voice now. 'The summer still tends upon my state. And I do love thee. Therefore, go with me.'

That was Titania all over. She might love a man, but she was still going to get her own way, no matter what he wanted.

'I'll give you fairies to attend you,' she whispered, her voice rich with promise.

Bottom didn't look impressed.

'And they shall fetch you jewels from the deep,' she continued, stroking his long ears.

He looked a bit more interested.

'And sing while you sleep on pressed flowers. And I will get rid of your mortal grossness so that you can go like an airy spirit. Peaseblossom, Cobweb, Moth and Mustardseed!'

I sighed and tried to sound enthusiastic. 'Ready.'

'And I,' said Cobweb valiantly.

'And I,' said Moth. He seemed relieved that I was back and he didn't have to make any decisions.

'And I,' said Mustardseed resignedly, because, after all, what else could we do? Titania was our Queen.

'Where shall we go?' we chorused obediently, as we had done a hundred thousand times before.

Titania regarded us sternly. 'Be kind and courteous to this gentleman; hop in his walks and gambol in his eyes. Feed him with apricots and dewberries, with purple grapes, green figs, and mulberries. The honey-bags steal from the humble-bees ...'

It was Polchis all over again, I thought. Didn't the Queen realise that humans didn't just want sweets? How about an egg and lettuce sandwich? Or a pizza? Mushroom and haloumi maybe, or Gaela's House Special?

I'd never eat another House Special pizza (with or without anchovies) again, I realised. Or smell the yeasty scent of Gaela's kitchen.

'And for night-tapers crop the bees' waxen thighs,'

continued Her Majesty, all the while smiling dotingly at Bottom.

'That's going to take us months,' muttered Cobweb. 'Bees' knees take forever to comb.'

'And light the candles at the fiery glow-worm's eyes.'

'That glow-worm glow is phosphorescence,' muttered Mustardseed, carefully low so Her Majesty didn't hear. But she was too absorbed in Bottom to pay us much heed. 'You can't light a candle with phosphorescence.'

'You can if you have a match too,' offered Moth.

Cobweb glared at him. 'If you have a match, you don't need the glow-worms.'

'But —' began Moth.

'Oh, be quiet,' snapped Mustardseed.

Titania kept murmuring orders to us, snuggling her blonde head into the hairy donkey's neck. 'Pluck the wings from painted butterflies to fan the moonbeams from his sleeping eyes. Nod to him, elves, and do him courtesies.'

Well, we could do all that, though it was going to be hard on the butterflies, even with anaesthetic. Maybe I could find them some prosthetic wings in exchange. Had anyone invented prosthetics for butterflies? Perhaps Titania wouldn't notice if we used painted cardboard wings instead of the real thing. I was pretty sure she wouldn't, not when she was as besotted as this.

At least the courtesies were easy. In Fairyland you learned those from the day you were born.

I bowed low before Bottom, waving my hand in true courtier fashion. 'Hail, mortal!'

'Hail!' echoed Cobweb gallantly.

Moth gave a double salute, then bowed too. 'Hail!' He really seemed to mean it.

'Hail!' sighed Mustardseed.

Bottom gave a donkey grin. I guessed no one had ever bowed to him before. 'I cry your worship's mercy, heartily,' he said. 'I beseech your worship's name.'

'Cobweb,' said Cobweb.

'I shall desire you of more acquaintance, good Master Cobweb. If I cut my finger, I shall use you to stop the bleeding.' Bottom turned to me. 'Your name, honest gentleman?'

I pulled up a dutiful smile from somewhere near my ankles. 'Peaseblossom,' I said, remembering how I'd told Gaela my name was Pete. What would my life have been like if I really was a Pete? I wondered. But no … Pete or Peaseblossom, it would have been just the same. I would still have been a fairy, bound to obey the King and Queen.

Bottom nodded to me solemnly. 'I pray you, commend me to Mistress Squash, your mother, and to Master Peapod, your father. Good Master Peaseblossom, I shall desire you of more acquaintance too.'

He turned to Mustardseed, who was concentrating on fanning his wings quickly so he didn't grin at the wrong time. 'Your name, I beseech you, sir?' Bottom enquired.

'Mustardseed,' said Mustardseed, with a flourish of his hand.

'Good Master Mustardseed, I know your skills well,' said Bottom. 'That same cowardly, giant-like ox-beef has devoured many a gentleman of your house: I promise you your kindred made my eyes water ere now. I desire your more acquaintance, good Master Mustardseed.'

Did he realise he was offering to eat Mustardseed, or at least his friends and family? I sighed again, then pretended it was a yawn when Titania glared at me.

'Come, wait upon him,' she ordered me. 'Lead him to my bower.'

Titania looked lovingly at Bottom again, then added to Moth, 'Tie up my love's tongue and bring him silently.'

Doting or not, Queen Titania was getting tired of Bottom's attempts at declaiming too.

Moth took a tiny vial from his belt and dripped some of its contents into Bottom's eyes. Then we each gathered an arm or leg and lugged the weaver across the glade to the mossy flowered bank we'd brought in for the Queen.

Titania had already stretched herself out on it. She held out her arms to Bottom. 'Come, sit thee down upon this flowery bed,' she ordered. 'While I your amiable cheeks do coy, and stick musk-roses in thy sleek smooth head, and kiss your fair large ears, my gentle joy.'

Bottom lay back, his hairy donkey head in her lap. She kissed his long ears. He wriggled as though it tickled.

'Where's Peaseblossom?' he demanded.

So much for a potion to make him silent. I glared at Moth.

'Sorry,' he whispered. 'I think I gave him cough drops instead of silence.'

Titania was already raising an eyebrow at me, in the way an army might raise its weapons.

'Ready,' I sighed.

'Scratch my head, Peaseblossom,' ordered Bottom. 'Where's Monsieur Cobweb?'

'Ready,' said Cobweb, sounding resigned.

'Monsieur Cobweb, good monsieur, get you your weapons in your hand, and kill me a red-hipped humble-bee on the top of a thistle. And, good monsieur, bring me the honey-bag. Do not fret yourself too much in the action, monsieur. And, good monsieur, have a care the honey-bag break not. I would not want to have you overflown with a honey-bag, signor. Where's Monsieur Mustardseed?'

'Ready.' Mustardseed was trying not to giggle at the weaver attempting to sound like a king. Titania gave him a look that would make a plunging meteor head back up into space.

'Give me your neaf, Monsieur Mustardseed. Pray you, leave your courtesy, good monsieur,' said Bottom, making no sense at all.

Still, Mustardseed looked enthusiastically obedient. 'What's your will?'

Titania smiled and went back to threading roses into Bottom's pelt.

'Nothing, good monsieur,' replied Bottom, 'but to help Sir Cobweb to scratch.' He raised a hand to touch his donkey chin, looking puzzled. 'I must to the barber's, monsieur, for I feel marvellous hairy about the face. And I am such a tender ass, if my hair tickles me, I must scratch.'

Cobweb and Moth fluttered above Bottom's head so they could scratch his long ears.

'Will you hear some music, my sweet love?' murmured Titania adoringly.

Bottom nodded. 'I have a reasonable good ear in music.'

Two very big ears, I thought. How long would Oberon let this go on? Puck should have said something, or even stopped it, as soon as Titania had seen Bottom. After ten thousand years in Oberon's service, he must have some influence on the King.

'Let's have the tongs and the bones,' suggested Bottom.

Titania blinked. It was obvious she had no idea what kind of music tongs and bones would make, nor did she want to find out.

'Or say, sweet love, what you desire to eat,' she added hurriedly.

'Truly, a peck of provender,' said Bottom, cheering up at the thought of food. 'I could munch your good dry oats. I have a great desire to a bottle of hay too: good hay, sweet hay, there's nothing like it.'

Titania beckoned Cobweb. 'I have a venturous fairy that shall seek the squirrel's hoard, and fetch thee new nuts,' she told Bottom. It was as if she hadn't heard the words 'hay' or 'oats'.

Love is blind, I thought, and deaf. Or enchanted love is, at any rate.

'I had rather have a handful or two of dried peas,' said Bottom, yawning. 'But, I pray you, let none of your people stir me. I have an exposition of sleep come upon me.'

Titania smiled and stroked his donkey nose. 'Sleep, and I will wind you in my arms.' She waved her hand at us. 'Fairies, be gone.'

We vanished obediently, though I went only as far as the branch of an olive tree at the edge of the glade. I made myself as small as a bee again.

This has to be put right, I thought, listening to Titania murmuring to the sleeping Bottom, 'O, how I love you! How I dote on you!'

She laid her blonde head on his dark hairy one. Her curls glowed like the beams of moonlight that had kissed Gaela's wet hair.

I shoved the thought away.

At last Titania slept too. I took a deep breath. At least she couldn't get into more trouble while she slept.

My first job was to find Puck, get more potion, then cure Lysander.

CHAPTER 12

I TAPed into Puck's office glade in Fairyland. He wasn't there. I TAPed again, this time to the ring of mushrooms where Puck lived. I glanced at the mushroom that I'd soon be moving into with Flossie. She'd already arranged a fence of long white teeth around it, and a shiny white path leading to the door.

But it was Puck's mushroom I needed now. I hammered on the door in its stem.

It creaked open. An elderly fairy with a purple face wearing a tattered yellow and green dressing gown blinked at me. 'What do you want?'

'Fairy Daffodil?' I stammered.

She wiped away a bit of what I now saw was a facemask. 'Who do you think I am, Peaseblossom? Sir George and the dragon?'

Actually she looked a bit like a dragon, with a touch of St George too.

'I've hardly had a wink of sleep since spring,' she grumbled. 'Do you think it's easy painting every blinking flower as soon as it pokes up from the earth?'

'Er, no.'

'Thank goodness for snowdrops. Why can't humans be content with white? But, no. They want yellow, pink, red, blue. If I see one more bluebell wood, I'm going to puke!'

'I'm looking for Puck,' I said.

Her sulky face glowed at the mention of her husband. See, love potion *did* make people happy. Even Fairy Daffodil.

'He's down in the workshop,' she said, standing aside to let me in. 'Good job with the Hippolyta and Theseus wedding, by the way,' she added.

'Thanks.' I brushed past her and clattered down the steps to the cellar. 'Puck, it's all gone —'

'To gryphon dung. I know!' Puck looked up from the bench. Something vaguely pink bubbled in a jar in front of him. 'I've got to put it right! Oberon was expecting a potion to undo the charm on the Queen ten seconds ago, and another for Lysander and Demetrius.'

'But love potion is permanent!' I said.

If it wasn't, there'd be fairies experimenting with it every few days — in love here, infatuated there …

'Oberon says it isn't. That's why he used it on Titania. He says that about a thousand years ago I found an antidote.'

'Did you?'

'Yes.'

I sagged in relief. 'You take it to Oberon then, and I'll find the lovers in the wood.'

'But I can't remember it!' wailed Puck.

'Oh.'

'I've made potions by the hundreds in the last thousand years. Curing flatulence, turning doves grey —'

'People still fart,' I interrupted.

'They weren't all successful,' Puck said sulkily. 'But this one was. There was this prince riding to his wedding — charming bloke — but a girl called Snow White needed to be kissed to dislodge a piece of poisoned apple … Long story. Anyway, two drops of anti-love potion and he forgot all about his waiting bride. Then two drops of heartsease, and two more for Snow White, and nine months later the two kingdoms were united and she'd had triplets.'

'What about the other bride?' I asked. 'The one waiting for the charming prince?'

'That's where the rest of the anti-love potion went. The jilted bride was really annoyed, what with all the wedding presents to send back and everything. She snatched the jar out of my hand. What was her name again ...'

'We have to go back and get it!' I said.

'But I can't remember when all this happened.'

'Okay, let's calm down.' I shoved him onto a stool. 'Where did all this happen?'

'Sarmatia, about a thousand years ago, give or take a hundred. Amaz — that was the jilted bride's name.'

I sat down too. The pieces were coming together. A woman furious with the man who'd abandoned her ... armed with a potion to make anyone fall out of love.

'Amaz started the Amazons,' I realised. 'She used your anti-love potion to form an army of women who couldn't fall in love.'

Puck's two currant eyes stared at me from his wrinkled-apple face. 'But Amazons fall in love — look at Hippolyta's warriors. Half her army are marrying Athenians now.'

'They don't need the potion any more — their tradition is established. But it was necessary in the beginning.'

I stood. 'Right. We head back to Sarmatia a thousand years ago. And we keep going back till we find Amaz. You can analyse the potion, and I'll make some more.' I took a deep breath. 'And then we'll split time like no one ever has before and get to Oberon ten seconds ago.'

'But it takes me forty minutes to girdle the earth!'

I grinned. 'I can do it in forty milliseconds, Great-Grandpa.'

Puck smiled. 'That's my boy.'

The air smelled of cocoa with a touch of cinnamon. Then it faded and horse dung and wildflowers took its place. Puck and I fluttered in the pollen-thick air above a world that was all grass. Long golden grasslands that reached to the horizon, dappled with white or yellow flowers, and with long-legged, tan-coloured horses grazing contentedly. The village huts nearby were made of grass too: long strands plaited together, then woven tightly over bent saplings. They were brown, not gold, but without the smoke from their cooking fires, they'd have been hard to see.

Two children ran past us. They had blonde hair, leather trousers, tiny bows slung over their backs and a quiver each full of miniature arrows. Amazons started training young. Both girls, of course. I didn't want to think what happened to male children here.

The girls stopped and stared at the two small fairies hovering above the grass.

'Bee time!' hissed Puck.

The girls blinked as we appeared to vanish, looked at each other, shrugged and ran on.

Puck and I buzzed towards the village, where women sat on wooden stools sharpening their twin-bladed axes, fletching arrows, trimming feathers. There were young, middle-aged and old women, most with battle scars, and some with wooden legs or hooks for hands to replace limbs lost in battle.

A couple of cowed-looking young men fetched more wood for the fire from a big pile of logs that must have been dragged there by the horses — or maybe a team of men. A youth milked one of the two horses in a small fenced area, while another squeezed honey from a comb into a leather bucket. There were no old men to be seen. I wondered whether, just like in a beehive, old males were killed when they were of no more use. Or maybe they were sent home to their villages after a few years of servitude, taking any boy children with them. I hoped it was that.

Suddenly one of the women yelled triumphantly and pointed. Three horses galloped into the village, a dead goat draped over one, the other two carrying female hunters with blood on their hands. The women slid off their horses and held their hands out for the men to bring water for them to wash.

'Is one of those women Amaz?' I whispered to Puck as we hovered above them.

'No. Though that second hunter has a look of her. Maybe we haven't gone far enough back.'

'We need to keep searching then,' I hissed. 'Come on!'

'Wait!' Puck flapped one of his bee's wings at an old, old woman sitting on a throne-like chair outside the biggest hut. The only hair left on her brown-spotted head were a few strands of grey, and her face was more wrinkled than a year-old rose petal. You could still see the strength in her face, but she was no young bride.

Puck hovered over the old woman's head and waved one of his bee legs at me. I flew over to him.

'This is Amaz,' he buzzed softly.

'Her?' But of course she'd have got old, I thought, as the old were once young.

I gazed down at her almost bald head, at the prominent veins in her legs below her knee-length leather skirt, then looked around the village — at the strong and happy working women, the laughing female hunters, the girls already stripping the hide from the goat, the silent men now fixing up a spit to cook it on. Amaz had created all this, all because she'd been jilted on her wedding day because of Puck and his anti-love potion and Oberon's fancy to see a charming prince waken an enchanted maiden.

Did Puck feel guilty? I wondered. But he was acting on Oberon's order. And the Amazon women looked happy, strong, healthy and fulfilled. The men, not so much. 'There it is!' Puck's squeak was almost loud enough for human ears.

The old woman tilted her head, as if hearing a sound almost forgotten, then smiled and looked back at the working women.

The flask sat in a position of honour on a tall wooden stand, the hut's only furniture except for the fur-covered bed. I peered inside it.

'It's empty. The potion's evaporated or been used up. There's just a bit of a green stain in the bottom.'

'Haven't I taught you anything, boy? I can analyse the dregs once I get it back home. Grab it!'

'How? I'm a bee.'

'Then un-bee!'

To bee, or not to bee? I wouldn't be at all if the Amazons saw a strange man in their queen's hut. But there was no choice. I flicked to my full size and grabbed the flask.

'Come on!' I yelled to Puck.

'I can't!' I could hardly hear his terrified buzzing. 'There must be a beehive around here. The queen bee must have followed us in. She's ... attached herself to me ...'

And a drone who mated with a queen bee would soon be very, very dead. That meant I'd be promoted to Puck's job straight away — but family was family, and, nuisance that he could be at times, I loved old Puck.

'The potion!' he buzzed. 'Spray the queen bee with the anti-love potion.'

'The flask is as dry as the Sphinx's armpits,' I told him. 'Change back, old man.'

I mean, it was obvious.

'Oh. Right.' The words were said in human form — and loud enough to attract the attention not just of Amaz but the warriors too.

Someone gave a scream of rage, which turned into a war yell, which was followed by shouts of delight as the women grabbed their battle axes.

It was time to TAP.

CHAPTER 13

We landed with a thump in Puck's workshop. I reached for the spectrometer I'd given him as a Midsummer's Eve present last year. (He'd given me a tricycle. Sometimes he didn't quite remember how old his descendants were.)

Puck pushed my hand away. 'I may be old,' he grumbled, 'but my nose can still tell me more than your modern gadgets can.' He took a deep sniff of the flask. 'Elderberry, two parts; rosehip, one part; hawthorn berry, two parts; bitter aloe, four parts; a drop of rosemary juice; three drops of sage; a leaf of lemon myrtle.'

I flicked through time on the last syllable. A girdle around the world in forty milliseconds — I had broken the speed of sound! The world was still rumbling as

I arrived back in Puck's lab surrounded by a mist of single origin 75% cocoa dark chocolate.

'Got it!' I yelled, throwing every ingredient into the juice extractor. I poured half the juice into a flask and the other half into another flask that I shoved into a pouch on my belt.

'You give this first flask to Oberon so he can unenchant Her Majesty,' I told Puck. 'Get rid of that donkey idiot too. I'll find the lovers and unenchant them.'

I grabbed Puck's hand and dragged him back into the rumbling neverwhen. We broke the sound barrier, the speed of light, and then the time barrier, all in a haze of chocolate sultanas.

I found the four young lovers asleep in the wood. Not in an enchanted glade. Not in any glade at all, just some trees and a few briars and a lot of goat droppings. They looked as if they had dropped down, exhausted, after chasing around in a confusion of emotions and too many trees. Demetrius snored slightly, his hand reaching towards Helena's. Lysander lay close to Helena's other side. Hermia was by herself, a huddle of arms and legs and tunic, her head on a tree root, her face streaked with dust and tears. She even sobbed a little in her sleep.

I perched on a branch above them, fairy-sized, the bottle of potion in my belt pouch. All I had to do was drip a little anti-love potion in Lysander's eyes and all would be well; he would love Hermia once more in the morning. And Demetrius could keep his enchanted infatuation with Helena. I could make things doubly sure by dropping love potion in Helena's eyes in case she ever noticed, or began to care, that she'd married a brute. And maybe some love potion in Lysander's eyes too, at the moment he first saw Hermia again ...

The branch rocked slightly as Puck landed next to me. 'Done the job yet?'

'Not yet. How is Her Majesty?'

'Awake and perfectly happy. She's forgotten all about the human, donkey ears and all. Oberon spirited off her pageboy while she was asleep, but she didn't even notice.' Puck yawned. 'It's going to be a decent Midsummer's Eve revels after all. I remember the first time I was in charge — Oberon had heard about a music group called The Beatles, and I thought he said beetles.' He stopped and peered at me. 'What's wrong, boy?'

I waved at the sleeping humans. 'All this. Why do we meddle?'

He spoke seriously for once. 'Some of what we do is good, boy. The world would be awash with teeth if it weren't for fairies like your Flossie; and spring would be as washed out as the weaver's old trousers if not for my Daffodil and her gang. And many a young girl would go wrong without the Fairy Godmother Regiment.'

'But enchanting people ... Have you ever thought what their lives would be like if we left them to choose freely?'

'Of course,' Puck said quietly. 'I've lived and served ten thousand years, boy. Of course I've wondered.'

'Maybe Theseus had a woman he loved — or who at least loved him — back in Athens,' I said. 'And Hippolyta — no Amazon marries. She's been forced into something she'd never have chosen.'

'You sure about that? Theseus and Hippolyta have more in common than you might think. Both magnificent leaders. Both prepared to give their lives for their people. He respects her. She admires him. I don't think they'd have found anyone else they'd feel like that about. It's not a bad basis for a life together, potion or not.'

'And if I hadn't used the potion, one would have killed the other and then perhaps mourned all their life for something they didn't realise they'd lost,' I said, trying to convince myself. Then I shook my head. 'It still wasn't right.'

'I know, boy.'

I stared at him. 'You agree?'

'It wasn't right. But I don't think it matters much either. You think people really want to choose their own destinies?'

'They don't get a chance,' I said bitterly. 'We do what Their Majesties order. So did the Athenians and the Amazons.'

'But it's not like that in a few thousand years. Things change.' He gave me a sharp look. 'I know you've flicked yourself far into the future a few times. I did too for a while, when I was young.'

'Why did you stop?'

'Because in the future, humans have free choice — some of them at least,' he said quietly. 'They have all we can never have: they can marry who they want, take whatever job they want, even dress as they wish. And what do they do with all the freedom? They get computers to match them up romantically; and wear whatever a few fashion designers decide is the next "new black". Most of them are like a horde of gryphons, all following the leader, taking the jobs they're expected to take. Even though they're free to dream, to make their own choices, they prefer to do work someone else tells them to do, and take holidays someone else has dreamed up for them.'

'Not all of them,' I said. I could have added, 'Once, a long time in the future, there was a selkie who chose to mix flour and water into dough, who sacrificed everything to make the best pizza in the world.' But I didn't. For even Gaela had chosen to go back to selkie life again.

'I'd better give the humans the anti-love drops,' I said instead. 'They'll be waking up soon.'

I flew down from the branch and squeezed a good helping of anti-love juice into Lysander's eyes, then moved his head slightly so it would be Helena he saw when he woke.

I hesitated, then left Demetrius alone and flew back up to Puck.

'All will be well,' he said.

'Yes, all will be well,' I repeated dully, just as a mob of long-legged dogs bounded through the trees, then stopped to sniff the sleepers.

I could hear Hippolyta's voice. She sounded happy, even excited.

'I was with Hercules and Cadmus once,' she said, 'when in a wood of Crete they bay'd the bear with hounds of Sparta.'

She came nearer, arm in arm with Theseus. A handful of their court followed them at a discreet distance.

I recognised Egeus and grinned. Too bad, old grump, I thought. This wasn't going to be a good day for fathers who ordered their daughters to marry their drinking mates.

'Never did I hear such gallant chiding,' Hippolyta continued. 'For, besides the groves, the skies, the fountains, every region near seem'd all one mutual cry. I never heard so musical a discord, such sweet thunder.'

Theseus smiled at her. Yes, I thought, there was genuine admiration for a warrior there, as well as the enchanted love. He'd never have found a woman like Hippolyta among the ladies of his court with their primped hair and their jewels and soft silk slippers. She could even declaim beautifully and, trust me, most declaimers didn't.

'My hounds are bred out of the Spartan kind,' Theseus informed her. 'Their heads are hung with ears that sweep away the morning dew.'

He wasn't bad at declaiming either, I thought.

'Crook-kneed, and dew-lapped like Thessalian bulls,' he continued. 'Slow in pursuit, but matched in mouth like bells, each under each. A cry more tuneable was never hollaed to, nor cheered with horn, in Crete, in Sparta, nor in Thessaly. Judge when you hear —' He stopped as he noticed the sleeping lovers. 'But, soft! What nymphs are these?'

Egeus stumped forward. 'My lord,' he yelped, sounding like a toad someone had sat on, 'this is my daughter here asleep! And this, Lysander!'

For a moment I thought Egeus was going to kick Lysander in the ribs. Then he noticed the others.

'This is Demetrius,' he said wonderingly. 'And here's Helena, old Nedar's Helena. I wonder of their being here together.'

Theseus exchanged a glance with Hippolyta. They both obviously had exactly the same idea about why young lovers might sneak out into the wood at night.

Theseus grinned, then patted Egeus soothingly. 'No doubt they rose up early to observe the rite of May, and hearing our intent, came here to grace our solemnity.'

Egeus didn't look convinced; even he wasn't that dim-witted. But how could he contradict his king?

Theseus winked at Hippolyta, then added quickly,

'But speak, Egeus. Is not this the day that Hermia should give answer of her choice?'

'It is, my lord,' said Egeus, glad to be self-righteous again.

Theseus gazed at the four sleepers. One of the hounds lifted its leg on Demetrius, but he didn't wake.

'Go, bid the huntsmen wake them with their horns,' Theseus said, just as another dog began to lick Helena's face. She woke with a shriek.

The others stirred, then sat, rubbing their eyes. I saw the moment when they stopped trying to work out where they were or why they were there, and realised that all that mattered this second was that they were lying down in the presence of royalty and could be beheaded for such disrespect.

Hermia clambered to her feet first. She gave Lysander a cautious glance. He gave her a reassuring half-smile back. Hermia bit her lip, obviously longing to speak, but unable to with royalty gazing at her, not to mention her enraged father.

Theseus grinned at the rumpled foursome with twigs in their hair and prickles in their clothes. 'Good morrow, friends. Saint Valentine is past: begin these wood-birds but to couple now?'

'Pardon, my lord,' said Lysander, trying to look as if such an activity had never crossed his mind.

'I pray you all, stand up,' Theseus told the still prone Helena and Demetrius, trying not to laugh as Demetrius noticed the wet patch on his tunic. Then he looked from Demetrius, now sniffing the stain and obviously hoping it was dew, to Lysander. He said more seriously, 'I know you two are rival enemies. How comes this gentle concord in the world, that hatred is so far from jealousy, to sleep by hate, and fear no enmity?'

Lysander shook his head. 'My lord, I shall reply amazedly, half sleep, half waking. But as yet, I swear, I cannot truly say how I came here. But, as I think,' he glanced at Hermia, a glance of love and determination, then raised his chin, 'for truly would I speak, and now do I bethink me, so it is — I came with Hermia hither. Our intent was to be gone from Athens, safe from the peril of the Athenian law.'

Egeus gave a small scream of rage and turned to Theseus, all righteousness and fury. 'Enough, enough, my lord, you have enough! I beg the law, the law, upon his head. They would have stolen away. They would, Demetrius, thereby to have defeated you and me, you of your wife and me of my consent, of my consent that she should be your wife.'

Demetrius looked up from the stain on his tunic. He'd obviously given up hoping it was dew. Then he noticed Helena staring at him with her puppy eyes. His face softened just a little.

He looked back at Theseus. 'My lord, fair Helena told me they would creep away through this wood. And I in fury followed them,' he admitted. 'Fair Helena followed me.' He shook his head wonderingly. 'But, my good lord, I know not by what power — but by some power it is — my love to Hermia, melted as the snow, seems to me now ...'

Oh, great, I thought. Another declamation. And Demetrius's verbiage was almost as bad as Bottom's.

'... as the remembrance of an idle gaud,' continued Demetrius, obviously proud of his turn of phrase, 'which in my childhood I did dote upon. And all the faith, the virtue of my heart, the object and the pleasure of mine eye, is only Helena. To her, my lord, was I betrothed ere I saw Hermia: but, like in sickness, did I loathe this food. But, as in health, come to my natural taste, now I do wish it, love it, long for it, and will for evermore be true to it.'

Demetrius took Helena's hand, bowed over it, then kissed it. Helena blinked, then gave a cautious smile.

Hermia moved closer to Lysander. They put their arms around each other and looked defiantly at their king, the courtiers and Hermia's father.

I held my breath. If Theseus decided to put Hermia to death for refusing to marry Demetrius, I suspected Lysander would follow her, whether it was to be burned at the stake or walled up in a cave.

Theseus looked at Hippolyta again. She smiled at him. To my surprise there was the love glow and respect of equals and friends between them, as well as the enchantment.

Puck nudged me. 'Told you so,' he whispered.

Theseus gave a rueful shrug. He would do what his lady so obviously wished.

'Fair lovers,' he began, 'you are fortunately met. Egeus, I will overbear your will; for in the temple at our wedding these couples shall eternally be knit too.'

Excellent! Three human marriages to begin the Midsummer's Eve revels. Titania would be delighted.

'And, for the morning now is something worn,' Theseus went on, 'our purposed hunting shall be set aside. Away with us to Athens; three and three, we'll hold a feast in great solemnity. Come, Hippolyta.'

The dogs galloped away in front, as good hunting dogs did. Theseus and Hippolyta followed, hand in hand;

then Demetrius, gallantly arm in arm with Helena, and Egeus hobbling next to him, obviously hoping to change Demetrius's mind — and the King's — before he got a son-in-law he loathed. Hermia and Lysander came next. They looked tired and dazed; she had prickles in her hair, and his hands and face had been scratched by brambles. But you could have woven another sun out of their happiness.

At last they were all gone. Puck yawned and stretched, then flexed his wings.

'Time for a nap,' he said. 'You'd better get a few zzzs too, before the revels tonight. You want to be fresh for your wedding. Ah, I remember mine ... an arch of jonquils, bluebells and anemones ...'

'Our arch will be pliers held by Tooth Fairies,' I said.

'You'll be happy,' he promised. 'Trust me, boy. You will love her all your life.'

'I know,' I said. That was the worst thing of all.

CHAPTER 14

Puck flew off, still yawning. I stayed where I was, sitting on the branch, letting the breeze stroke my wings. It smelled of dogs and olive trees. It smelled real.

Soon I'd be back in Fairyland, surrounded by the scents of honeysuckle and roses, Dew Brew and whatever flower the Queen fancied this week. It would be beautiful. It always was. But I couldn't haul up the energy to TAP myself over there. It had been quite a week. Or ten thousand years, whichever way you wanted to look at it.

Suddenly someone came tramping under the trees nearby. I peered through the branches. It was Bottom, the weaver, with his own head now, which was an improvement unless you were fond of donkeys. I've always liked donkeys.

Bottom was presumably off to the Athenian palace to join his friends in the play for Theseus and Hippolyta's wedding. He looked a bit confused and not terribly happy.

'Sir Bottom!' I called.

He blinked at me as I fluttered down to him. 'Monsewer Peasebottom ... I thought you were just a dream. Such a dream I thought I had, yet here you are. Monsewer Peasebottom —'

'Peaseblossom,' I corrected him.

'Ah, methought perchance we were related.' He looked even more despondent. 'So that was not a dream last night? The woman with the lustrous hair a-stroking me? For if it were real, I am not sure what my wife will say.'

He wasn't very bright, but he didn't deserve what had been done to him.

'Don't worry,' I said. 'It was a dream. It still is. Midsummer is the time for dreams.'

'Ah, good,' he said, still looking at me warily as I fluttered at his eye height.

'Sir Bottom, what would you have if you could choose anything in the world?' I asked. I hoped it would be something fairy gold could buy.

'Why, sir,' he said readily, with no need to ponder the question, 'I would like to love my job. I am a weaver, the son of a weaver, journeyman to a weaver. I married a weaver's daughter when I were apprenticed to her father. All day I weave, except for feast days such as this. Weaving this week and the next —'

'I get the idea,' I said.

Bottom shook his head. 'But I do not love the craft. I cannot love it. Wool thread all day, and wool blankets at night. At times I fear I will drown in wool. I hate the smell of wool. I would make beauty in the world, Monsewer Peaseblossom, but how can I make beauty out of wool?'

'Have you a thread of wool about you, sir?'

I fluttered over the pouch on his belt while he pulled out a few strands of wool, dirty and knotted. He held them out to me.

'Look up,' I said, 'and open your eyes wide, then look straight down again at your hands.'

I pulled out my trusty flask of love potion, making sure it was the right one. Two drops, in his big brown eyes.

He looked down. 'Wool!' he exclaimed, as if he had never seen it before. He lifted the threads to his nose ecstatically. 'Wool! The scent of it, sir! The breath of it! You know what I'm going to do with this wool, Monsewer Peaseblossom?'

I stopped fluttering so he could look at me more easily. 'No, Sir Bottom.'

'I am going to dye it with saffron, and dye other threads with rose, and green and blue and silver too. I am going to weave a tapestry of wool, Monsewer Peaseblossom, telling of all my strange dreams of last night. A lady most passing fair.'

Which would probably please Titania, but put Oberon in another huff.

'How about a tapestry showing the marriage of King Theseus to his Hippolyta instead?' I suggested. 'I imagine they would hang it in the palace's great hall for the whole court to gaze on.'

'You think they might?'

'With your love of wool, Sir Bottom, I am sure they will. People will speak of the wedding for ten thousand years, having seen the story of it in your work.'

'Then I must away!' he yelled. 'The play's the thing, to catch the attention of the King.'

Bottom was never going to make a poet. Or an actor. But he would truly be a weaver now, and a happy one. And I already knew that the story of Theseus's wedding would be told in ten thousand years.

Ten thousand years to Gaela's pizza shop ...

I could split time. Visit her café just once more, in disguise, long before she ever met me. Hear her voice, watch the wriggle of her seaweed tattoo. I might even sit on the shore, fairy-sized, and watch her make a delivery through the moonlit waves to the sea serpent.

But I wouldn't. I was a fairy, the son of a fairy, as Bottom was the son of a weaver. I would do my duty, and be as happy as Bottom was now.

It was time for Theseus and Hippolyta's wedding, and the weddings of the two couples I had just untangled.

Oberon would dance with Titania again at the Midsummer's Eve revels, happy to have stolen away her pageboy. She had forgotten poor little Polchis already.

And then I would be married too.

CHAPTER 15

Day Zero had come. This afternoon the Fairy Court would watch the human weddings, then, as dusk settled its softness on the land, we would begin the revels in Fairyland. Midsummer was the most propitious day for weddings, for fairies as well as humans. Queen Titania had decreed it.

I fluttered here and there, supervising everything. But I'd done my work well. The feasting glade was decked out with rosebuds, dew-drop diamonds, and carpeted half a metre deep with moss sprinkled with keep-it-green potion. The glow-worms and fireflies were ready in their barns, well-fed and watered and resting for their efforts tonight. Elvis had a sore throat, but nothing that a thyme and honey potion couldn't cure. A team of trained gryphons had dragged in the two thrones — Titania's a single vast carved ruby, Oberon's of emerald, both trimmed with gold. And I'd undone Moth's mistakes — he'd ordered fire-breathing dragons instead of glow-worms.

The feast itself was Cobweb's duty. You could always rely on Cobweb, so I just peeked into the royal kitchens. Fairy bread was baking, candied rosebuds were laid out for their final drying, crystallised violets winked like the tiny stars had above the ocean, as Gaela held my hand and drew me through the waves ...

I blinked back to reality, dashed to my foxglove and changed into a fresh rose-petal kilt, picked up a garland of flowers for my hair that had been left by the foxglove's stem and flew back to the feasting glade.

Puck hovered there already. He'd changed too; his blue doublet was immaculate and three blue armbands indicated his rank. I fluttered a few metres back from him out of respect, but near enough to lend a wing if he made a mistake.

He grinned at me. 'Going to be a fine revels, boy. One you'll never forget.'

I nodded. It was hard not to feel excited despite my sorrow at losing the ... the ... At losing a courageous friend who made stunning pizza.

'Showtime!' yelled Puck, his wings quivering.

Sixty fairy trumpeters marched into the glade. They lined up either side of it, then raised the stamens of their nasturtium trumpets and blew. The 'March of the Fairy Godmothers' rang through the forest.

I flew a little higher to get a better view. Here came the Fairy Godmother Regiment, squad after squad of them, each wearing her own shade of pumpkin with the insignia of their corps on her wand. Their glass slippers clacked in time to the music.

Next came the Flower Fairies, soaring towards us on their butterflies, Fairy Daffodil in the lead. She saluted Puck formally, then blew him a kiss and led her squadron to the far end of the glade.

The trumpeters broke into the 'Tooth Fairy Tango'. I thought I could make out the Fairy Floss among the blaze of shining white. Each held a toothbrush in one hand and pliers in the other, waving them at the growing crowd of fairies.

Titania's assorted court functionaries came next: Moth, Cobweb and Mustardseed and all the others, dressed in clean white rose-petal kilts; then Oberon's staff in their blue gryphon-skin doublets. I was looking forward to being awarded just such a uniform after my wedding tonight, as well as a blue double armband.

The cooks marched in, and then the hunters, mounted on their wasps. The trumpeters changed their wilted nasturtiums for new ones as Elvis marched into the glade alone, looking a bit like a vast Tooth Fairy himself in his white jumpsuit, smiling and waving, his sunglasses flashing in the sunlight. He stopped by the thrones. The trumpeters respectfully ceased their tweeting as he broke into 'Hound Dog'.

Finally Their Majesties flew in, hand in hand, their wings glistening in the sun. The Queen's dress was made of jewelled cobweb with the web itself removed. The King wore peacock spider silk, a thousand times more beautiful than anything made by silkworms.

They soared down and took their places on their thrones.

We all bowed, or curtsied, low.

'Rise!' cried Titania.

She looked as fresh as a rosebud despite her eventful night. There was no sign of Polchis. I guessed Oberon had the boy hidden away.

Oberon clicked his fingers. An image of the Athenian court appeared above the glade. The nobles wore their best leathers and linens — drab by fairy standards, but still impressive — golden necklaces and armbands and anklets and rings. Their spears, swords and battle axes had been left at home. Harpists strummed in the background. (There is no comparison between the music of a harp and that of a nasturtium trumpet. Trust me.)

Theseus entered, hand in hand with Hippolyta. Both wore purple tunics — hers long, but with a skirt split to allow easy movement; his knee-length — with soft leather boots, and golden coronets and armbands. It seemed Hippolyta had finally found a dress she could move in. Both she and Theseus looked as happy and triumphant as if they had found each other for themselves.

Elvis crooned softly in the background as the Fairy Court watched Theseus swear lifelong love to Hippolyta in front of both their peoples, which was how a royal wedding was performed at that time.

'Your honour shall be my honour,' said Theseus solemnly. 'Your people will be mine too.'

'And I vow to thee,' Hippolyta said, smiling and taking his hand, 'that I will love no other my whole life, nor give my life for any other, as long as I shall live.'

The Athenian King and his new Queen then sat on their thrones, which were carved from stone and inlaid with gold. Theseus must have had all his kingdom's carvers working solidly for the last two days to create a throne that exactly matched his.

Now, Theseus called Lysander and Hermia to come towards him and his new Queen. Lysander wore a simple white tunic with a small dark blue embroidered border. Hermia's dress was dark blue too, simple but finely woven.

Theseus gave the couple his royal blessing, then gestured for Hippolyta to do the same. Hippolyta spoke in her own tongue but the sentiment was the same: Lysander and Hermia were married. They looked terrified and triumphant, unsure yet irrevocably certain that this was the love their lives would encircle — which was the way the best of marriages began.

Egeus looked like he'd swallowed a python that had just eaten a bullock, but he had to pretend a smile when his king and queen looked at him.

Demetrius and Helena were married next. She must have been dreaming of her wedding day most of her life, for her dress showed the work of ten women embroidering for a decade. She seemed to me the kind of girl who was more in love with the wedding than her groom.

Demetrius wore red, which was as close as he could come to royal purple without being beheaded. He looked from side to side around the great hall to make sure that everyone was properly admiring him and his beautifully bedecked bride. But he looked happy, and so did she.

Slowly the Athenian sun sank like a vast burning ball, sending black shadows from the great rock across the plain. The Athenian court danced by torchlight, then sat on stools to watch the play. But by then our Fairyland Majesties were bored with mortal revels. It was, in truth, the most abysmal play.

Puck flicked off the image and its light was replaced by glow-worms inching about the royal glade, with fireflies dancing above. The moon shone down as brightly as it had the night a selkie took me by the hand and drew me deep into the ocean. But I should not think of that.

Then came another thought: yes, this night I *must* think of Gaela. Because tomorrow I would not remember her with love. I would not be able to think of her except with vague amazement that I had once found a selkie lovely. I would probably not even long for pizza.

Finally I could admit that I did love Gaela. A true and unsought love that I could never express to her; or to myself except in this moment when it was too late to condemn myself — and condemn her too. Because if I had chosen to spend my life with Gaela, Queen Titania would surely have punished her as wrathfully as she did me.

Gaela would be back under the green sea now, perhaps drifting into a sand-strewn cavern cool and deep, just as she had described, her dark hair swaying about her. Perhaps she had already rejoined the other selkies. They would welcome her back with ... What did selkies do for welcome? Would the wild white horses of the waves dance in joy that she had come home? I didn't know.

I knew almost nothing about selkies, and almost as little about Gaela, except the true sweet heart of her that I would love until ...

Until the heartsease drops were placed into my eyes.

'Peaseblossom!' a voice said. 'You are looking handsome. But your side petal is crooked.' Flossie fixed it with her small neat hands. 'Congratulations on the Athenian wedding, by the way. It was absolutely beautiful.'

'Thanks. You're looking lovely too.'

Flossie wore long chains of bright white baby teeth — like pearls but far more precious — looped about her neck; and her white petal dress was embroidered with small teeth as well. From a distance she was dressed like any other Tooth Fairy, but up close she was a bride.

She smiled at me. 'In another few minutes we'll be married. It doesn't seem quite real! Have you seen our mushroom today?'

I shook my head. 'I've been busy.'

'Your Great-Grandmother Daffodil planted snowdrops all about it, to match the teeth fence. So kind of her.' Flossie added in a whisper, 'Some of the lines of flowers weren't quite straight. Does she ...'

'Drink a bit too much Dew Brew? Yes, but only at midsummer.'

'I hope she brushes her teeth afterwards,' said Flossie. 'You should see the state some teeth get into. I'll give her a new toothbrush and some of my new anti-tartar mouthwash as a Midsummer's Eve present.' She smiled again, showing her pearly whites. 'I'll make sure you have all you need in the tooth department too, after we're married. Does it seem as strange to you?'

I managed a smile back. It wasn't Flossie's fault. She was a nice girl. Businesslike. Caring. Ambitious, just like me. 'I suppose it does for every fairy's wedding. What do a Tooth Fairy and a Potion Fairy have in common?'

'As much as Puck and Daffodil,' agreed Flossie, laughing. 'That's why we have the love potion.'

She took my hand. It was a good firm hand. She smelled of gardenias with just a hint of peppermint toothpaste. I would love that scent soon. Even now it was quite pleasant.

Their Majesties had chosen well for us. Two efficient fairies, happy together in their mushroom house, working at the jobs they loved, that they'd found fulfilling ever since Their Majesties had proclaimed they should.

'And now for my next number,' said Elvis.

That was the cue for the Fairy Orchestra to tune up; not just the trumpeters, but pipers too, with their hollow reed flutes, and drummers with hollyhock seedheads. The glow-worms moved to make a single glowing aisle leading to Their Majesties' thrones. The fireflies hovered above them.

Suddenly Puck was at my side. 'Big moment, boy. In a few minutes you'll be my permanent assistant.'

'And married,' I said.

'That too.'

He gave Daffodil a friendly squeeze as she walked past, glowing in her daffodil dress of lacy yellow cobwebs. She patted his cheek, then stood with the other Flower Fairies.

My parents were standing with Flossie's parents. They waved to us in a friendly fashion. Fairies lived too long to stay close to their parents; and of course baby fairies were brought up in a creche from one week old so our parents' work wasn't interrupted. It was quite rare to work with a relative, as I did with Puck. It was just coincidence, although I'd probably inherited his talent with potions.

Flossie took my hand as Elvis crooned 'Love Me Tender', and we walked together along the carpet of soft moss towards Their Majesties on their thrones.

Puck walked behind us, a jewelled flask of heartsease potion in his hand. I still had the potion flask from earlier in the pouch on my belt. With all the last-minute fuss I'd forgotten to remove it. But you didn't use ordinary potion flasks at a wedding.

Humans ask questions like: 'Do you love me?' 'Will you marry me?' 'Do you *still* love me?' But there's no need for questions like that before or after a fairy wedding. Why would there be when all weddings were ordained by the Fairy King and Queen?

King Oberon stood and took my hands. Titania stood and took Flossie's.

'She is yours, and yours to keep, till oceans dry and the sun weeps,' said Oberon to me.

'Love him till the seas run dry, love and never wonder why,' Titania commanded Flossie.

King Oberon gestured to Puck, who stepped forward.

'Do you take this potion willingly, to enchant you your whole life?' Puck asked Flossie.

'I do,' she said, and lifted her face so Puck could drip the potion into her eyes. She blinked, then gazed at me with such love that I felt my skin shiver.

Then it was my turn. I wiped my hands on my petalled kilt. For some reason I was sweating. All I had to do was yell 'No!' and … And what? No one had ever said no before. It was unthinkable. And yet I had thought it.

'Do you take this potion willingly, to enchant you your whole life?' Puck asked me.

Did I imagine it, or was there a faint warning note in his voice?

But there was no need of a warning. I lifted my face.

I had expected the drops to feel cold. Four hundred years of placing drops in others' eyes and I'd never known what they felt like. They were warm; their heat slipped through my veins. I was no longer the same; would never be the same; would never want to be the same.

I turned to Flossie. She smiled at me, radiant, loving and lovely, the face I would see every morning for the rest of my life, and every evening too, and each time with love.

I kissed her, and knew I could never be as happy again.

Behind us the Tooth Fairies laughed as they formed an arch, giggling and shoving. Tooth Fairies worked alone so they didn't have much experience in teamwork.

Flossie and I ran under the arch hand in hand, giggling, joyous, then took our places on the small thrones that Cobweb had placed at the other end of the glade from Their Majesties, where we would receive good wishes and our wedding presents.

The first gifts were a statue of a gryphon carved from moonstones from Oberon for our front garden; and a box of sugarplums that would never empty from Titania.

Flossie nudged me and muttered, 'Terribly bad for the teeth. But of course one can't tell Her Majesty that.'

I grinned at her. 'Certainly not!'

Puck and Daffodil gave us matching potion bottles made from gryphon teeth. Tasteful and useful. Daffodil kissed my cheek, then Flossie's.

We received a carpet woven from everlasting flowers from the Flower Fairies; a shower curtain made of slug teeth — very rare and nowhere near as slimy as you'd think; a set of fairy wands decorated with silver glitter;

a set of pumpkin-coloured sheets and towels from my Fairy Godmother; and another set in tooth-white from Flossie's. Some mushroom compost. You can never have too much mushroom compost, not if you don't want your living room to shrink. A toaster from Moth that would have been useful if mushrooms had electricity. A bag of mushroom spawn from Cobweb in case I wanted to grow a garden shed. Another bag of compost ...

All at once I could smell something. Something hot, with a hint of cheese and tomato sauce.

'Happy wedding,' said the creature hovering in front of me. It held out a gift.

It was a banshee. Without its partner, I couldn't tell if it was the female or male of the couple from the pizza shop, just a collection of black wisps with the hint of eyes.

Moth gasped. One of the Flower Fairies screamed. Flossie took my hand. Someone had hysterics near the Fairy Godmothers. Their Majesties glared.

I wondered if there had ever been a banshee at a fairy wedding before. The Midsummer's Eve revels were a time of total joy; and banshees only appeared to sing of death. Or to eat pizza.

I suddenly noticed the gift the banshee held among its whirling threads of black. A slice of ...

'Pizza?' asked Flossie, puzzled.

'Wedding present,' said the banshee hoarsely.

It handed the slice to me, then floated up to hover near an olive branch. At least the banshee wasn't singing, I thought vaguely. If it wasn't singing, then maybe no one was going to die.

I stared at the pizza wordlessly, then looked back at Flossie. 'I used to like pizza, long, long ago.' For that's what it seemed like now.

I could have said, 'I loved a girl who was a selkie, and whose hands smelled of yeasty pizza dough.' But I had never told Gaela that I loved her. A fairy wasn't free to say words like that.

Yet somehow I found myself standing.

'I loved a girl once,' I said to the assorted onlookers, and took a bite of pizza.

And suddenly, as I tasted the cheese and tomato, still hot, almost bubbling, it was as if Gaela was there, and all the patrons of the Leaning Tower of Pizza too, and the crusts were browning to exactly the right crisp in the oven, and the tomato sauce had chunks of fresh tomato in it, as well as basil and a hint of oregano, and there was laughter and happiness because the customers were eating the best pizza in the world. Even when they got home and the selkie charm had vanished, they would remember the taste of that pizza.

The banshee began to sing.

A quiet wail came from the Fairy Godmothers. They were a staunch lot, but they knew what a banshee's song meant. Some of the Tooth Fairies fainted. So did Elvis.

'Peaseblossom,' said Flossie faintly.

I kissed her cheek. 'It's all right. The banshee hasn't come for you, I'm fairly sure.'

And then the song took over. There was no way to describe a banshee melody. It was loss and it was joy, the saddest and most wonderful music in the world, for life was always the other side of death, just as loss was part of love.

But there was no death in Fairyland. Fairies just faded till they were almost too faint to see and were mostly forgotten. No one could die tonight, nor any time here. Unless ...

I stared up at the banshee as its song ended. It had almost vanished too, till it was just a black shape blocking out the stars. And then the stars shone bright again and the banshee was gone.

I might have dreamed it, were it not for the mutters all around me and the pizza in my hand.

Titania gestured to Cobweb, and Oberon glanced at Puck. Puck nodded. He and Cobweb hauled Elvis to his feet. Puck poured a little potion down his throat. I didn't know what kind, but it was purple and bubbled.

Elvis began to sing 'Love Me Tender' again.

'Peaseblossom?' Flossie said again, under the cover of the music. 'Are you all right?'

'I love you,' I said.

She smiled. 'I love you too.'

'But I shouldn't love you. It's like mixing … anchovies and ice cream. You shouldn't put anchovies on ice cream, and you shouldn't put one love onto another.'

'But … but you do love me,' she stammered, anguish shafting her eyes. For of course she loved me, and would love me till she died.

Unless the banshee had been right.

I took another bite of pizza.

'Yes, I love you,' I said. 'But I must still do this.'

I took the flask of anti-love potion out of the pouch on my belt. There were four drops left.

Something could die in Fairyland. It would die tonight. My love for Flossie and hers for me — the love that never should have been, or it would have been there all along.

'Flossie, please forgive me.'

I didn't want to hurt her. Not just because I loved her right now, but because I liked and respected her, and this would be painful for her, for a few seconds at least. It might embarrass her too. I hoped desperately that Their Majesties would blame me, not her.

Flossie looked at me lovingly and I could see she understood. Because she did love me, she loved me enough to want my happiness.

She leaned forward so I could put the drops into her eyes.

I smiled at her with love and joy one last time, because I loved her and because she deserved it, then put the last two drops into my own eyes.

And it was done.

'You idiot, Peaseblossom,' muttered Puck. He was the only one who understood what I'd done.

Except for Flossie of course, who was looking at me sympathetically. Her love for me had gone, but she still cared. She truly was a nice girl, but not the one for me. Nor was I the one for her.

No one else in the court knew an anti-love potion existed; except for Oberon, and he wasn't going to confess any of that to Titania.

'You can still fix this, boy!' Puck whispered urgently. 'Put more love drops in her eyes now, then drip them in yours. There's still time. If you're quick, Their Majesties will never guess what you've just done. Say you had a gnat in your eye or something.'

I looked around the glade. Oberon and Titania were discussing what the banshee's appearance meant. They weren't looking at us at all. Moth sat at Titania's feet giving her a foot rub. The fireflies were dancing, their glow adding to the enchantment of the moonlight. Everything was impeccable again. The moon was as round as a cheese, and it gave off so much light I could see a whole spectrum of colours …

'And that's what love is,' I murmured. 'A million different colours, constantly changing.'

'Peaseblossom!' hissed Puck.

'Do what you must,' Flossie whispered to me. She really was quite pretty. I was glad children's teeth were in such good hands.

'Love is seeing colours for the first time,' I announced to anyone who might be listening. 'It's feeling as if your soul has been washed clean so it can join with another's. Their happiness makes you happy, and yours makes them smile. Love is the stars singing, and the waves crooning deep below the sand-strewn ocean ...'

Elvis stopped singing.

Titania rose to her feet. 'What is going on here, Peaseblossom?' she demanded.

I bowed to her. 'I apologise, Your Majesty. But I'd rather be known as Pete.'

'Pete?' She frowned. 'That's no name for a fairy.'

'No, it isn't,' I said, meeting her eyes.

The Queen's eyes were smouldering charcoal now. 'You are mine. You have always been mine. You always will be! Admit it, Peaseblossom. Say, "Your Majesty, I am yours, forever."'

'No, Your Majesty. You may kill me or enchant me — but I belong to myself, and to the love that I choose freely.'

'You will love who I wish,' commanded Titania. Her eyes turned golden, the colour of bewitchment. 'You *will* be happy, Peaseblossom.'

It wasn't just a command. It was magic. Titania didn't need heartsease potion to make one fairy love another. I had never guessed at even half her power.

I felt love seeping back into me. Love for Flossie; an even greater love for Queen Titania. The enchantment froze my toes, my ankles, warming as it reached my knees.

I took another bite of pizza. The cheese was cold and soggy now, but it didn't matter. I felt Titania's enchantment slide away.

There was no magic in Gaela's pizza. Gaela wouldn't do that to her customers. Besides, good pizza didn't need magic. No, this was reality keeping the Fairy Queen's enchantment at bay.

Titania sensed her power over me drifting away, like the shattered debris of a shipwreck. She seemed puzzled. 'Peaseblossom, whatever you are doing, stop it! This is for your own good. The Fairy Floss will be the perfect wife for you.'

'Will she ever smell of seaweed?'

The Queen frowned. 'Of course not.'

'Then she can't be the perfect wife. Not for me.'

'Don't be ridiculous. Put more love potion into your eyes,' Titania ordered, her voice as cold as an iceberg, 'and in the Fairy Floss's eyes. You will love her forever, and she you. You will be happy, Peaseblossom, and not just in your marriage. I can give you all your heart desires.' It was a threat as much as a promise.

Queen Titania's eyes met mine. They were like sapphires now, if sapphires had learned to smile. Titania was the most beautiful woman in existence, with her golden hair, her skin like pearls, a glow to her every movement so her very essence seemed to carry through the air.

Except she wasn't. The most beautiful woman in existence had dark hair that drifted in the sea, and a tattoo of seaweed on her neck.

'You could have everything, Peaseblossom,' Titania murmured. 'I can give you the sun to play netball with, or the stars to juggle.'

She could too. But who wanted to juggle stars?

I bowed. 'Thank you, Your Majesty. But from now on I answer to the name of Pete.'

I turned to Flossie. She was a perfectly nice fairy and we'd have been happy together. But an enchanted love wasn't the kind I wanted.

'I'm sorry,' I said simply.

She smiled. A good smile, with straight white teeth and excellent gums. 'It doesn't matter,' she said kindly. And it didn't for her, not any more.

Titania gave me a look that could have shrivelled a volcano. I clutched what remained of my slice of pizza and thought of Gaela.

'Moth!' commanded the Queen. 'Change into bridal petals, now! We must have a wedding!' She gave me another withering glare. 'We will not let this fool spoil our revels.'

'I'm to marry the Fairy Floss?' squeaked Moth, looking both terrified and overjoyed.

'And you are promoted to Fairy Class 1, assistant to Puck.' Titania turned to me. 'As for you —'

'Get out of here fast, boy,' muttered Puck. 'Or you're going to be a toad for all eternity.'

'I'm going,' I said. And vanished.

CHAPTER 16

The world smelled vaguely of chocolate milkshake as I appeared in Oberon's main glade. My magic was fading; I only had a few minutes left at most. Maybe even seconds — though hopefully Titania would wait till Moth and Flossie were married, and everyone had sung and danced and given Moth the presents meant for me, before she decided what to do with me.

Would she let me live? Or make me vanish as if I had never been?

No, that would mean too much work, as she would need to clean up all traces of my actions.

Perhaps she would turn me into a beetle? That would be more like her. Or maybe an oyster, stuck to a rock, doomed to create the biggest, most uncomfortable pearl possible over the next few hundred years.

But while a shred of magic was left to me, I had a duty to do.

I gazed around the glade. Oberon's retinue were all at the revels of course, but I'd hoped he'd left Polchis here. Yet there was no sign of him; not a scent of sugarplum nor the cushion Titania had given him to sit upon.

I panicked, worrying I'd never find him in whatever time I had left. I had to calm down and think.

Of course! Titania had forgotten all about the boy while she was enchanted with Bottom, but Oberon would have wanted to make sure that if she did remember Polchis once the enchantment was lifted, she wouldn't be able to find him. Or glimpse him accidentally if she came to Oberon's glade. But where would Oberon have taken him? It could be anywhere in time and space.

I thought about it some more. It was unlikely Oberon would have gone to too much bother for a mere human boy. There was a hardly used glade behind the main one, used to store parchment and flasks and to recharge glow-worms. I flickered around a little in time and space, checking the glade in the present, the near past and almost future. By now my magic was barely strong enough to evoke even a whiff of milky cocoa.

Half the glow-worms in the back-room glade had lost their glimmer entirely, and there were even a few thistles among the clover flowers. Housekeeping probably hadn't even trimmed the honeysuckle for fifty years. But Polchis was there, sitting on a mossy log. (Moss doesn't need much maintenance if it is growing in the right spot.)

He'd cut a branch from a cherry tree, and was using his teeth to make a ridge in it so he could tie on the string he'd plaited from soft inner tree bark.

'Making a bow?' I asked, flying down and landing next to him. 'What will you do for arrows?'

Polchis jumped guiltily. 'I'm sorry, Sir Fairy. I won't do it again.'

'Make all the bows you want,' I said. 'The King and Queen have forgotten all about you.'

'Both of them? You're sure?'

I nodded. Titania would find a new pet — she always did. She loved anything new and glittery. And now Oberon had succeeded in taking Polchis from her, it was unlikely he'd ever think of him again. If either of them did remember him, they'd assume he was being trained to be an attendant somewhere. Or, as a short-lived human, he'd already died.

Polchis looked at the branch in his hand. 'It's not going to be a good bow. I've never been taught how to make one properly.'

'How about you learn today?'

'What do you mean?' he asked cautiously.

'I can take you home. To the exact moment you left. No one will even know you were gone.'

A hundred years had passed in his world in the few months he'd been in Fairyland, but I still had some time to play with time. I hoped.

'Or you can go anywhere else,' I offered. 'You could …' I tried to think what a human boy might want from life. 'You could be an astronaut and go to the Moon. Or be a fisherman. Or make pizza.'

'What's pizza?'

I realised I was still holding the remnant of the slice in my hand. It was cold by now, and the cheese was gluggy. I hesitated, then handed it to him.

The kid took a tentative bite, then wrinkled his nose.

'It's better hot,' I said.

'No, thank you.' He handed it back to me. 'I'd like to go home. Can I really?'

'I promise,' I said, then wondered if I could carry it out. What if Titania's revenge caught up with us between times? We might be lost in chocolate fumes forever, or even just cease to be. Should I tell him the risk and scare him? Or ...

Suddenly I could smell salt and seaweed. I even seemed to hear waves lapping at the pebbles.

I took Polchis's small hand in mine. 'It might be dangerous,' I said.

'I don't care!' He was only young, but he meant it.

And what did life offer him here? Happiness and sugarplums. Fairy gold with no substance.

I pulled the possibilities into place ... and smelled caramel chocolate, and cold, then suddenly warmth, and a strong scent of unfamiliar smoke and roasting meat.

I looked around. We had landed in the middle of a field of corn. No one could have seen us suddenly appear for the fat green stalks were half as tall again as me.

Polchis no longer wore his rose petals or flower garland, but a brown leather loincloth, soft leather shoes and a belt twisted around his waist. They must have been the clothes he was wearing when Titania snatched him up.

I nudged him. 'Off you go. I'll wait here to make sure it's all right.'

I expected him to run off straight away. Instead, he grabbed me around the legs and hugged me hard.

'Thank you, Mr Peaseblossom.'

I bent down in the soft dirt among the corn, muddying my white rose petals. 'Don't tell anyone what happened,' I warned him. 'Just think of the last few months as a dream. Go on with your life.' I smiled. 'Make it a good one.'

'Yes,' he said, just as a man's voice called, 'Polchis! Where are you?'

The kid grinned. It was as if the sun shone directly on his face. 'Here!' he yelled, and raced through the corn.

I peered out and saw a tall man wearing a leather skirt and feathered headdress swing the boy up onto his shoulders. Polchis yelled in delight, and the man trotted off towards the big fire in the middle of a circle of long leather-and-bark-covered houses. I saw women laughing together as they ground corn on big stones, or plucked ducks.

All this would vanish one day, I knew: this entire Native American kingdom gone, as if it had never been here. I saw too much sometimes, flying through time. Even the earth itself was only temporary: a small blue planet spinning in the darkness till its sun engorged and ate it, then faded to black too. Only the enchanted were unchanging.

But this was now, and it was real. Polchis was home.

My wings twitched. For a moment I thought they were caught in a spider's web, but then the tingle became a wrench, and then agony as each wing was slowly ripped from the skin and muscles of my back.

Titania had finally remembered me.

I only had seconds.

I bit my lip to stop myself screaming in agony, closed my eyes and thought of the Leaning Tower of Pizza. But it had gone, I remembered. There was no use even remembering it.

I thought instead of Gaela and her smile, and the smell of pizza with melted cheese, no anchovies. Tomato sauce, artichoke hearts, cubes of sautéed potato, basil leaves. Real ingredients. I gathered all my strength — it wasn't much — and felt time and place wobble about me, and then speed past.

I glimpsed a court where the women wore wide skirts ... a plague town with bodies piled high, and the few living hurrying by in strange masks ... a battlefield of mud and trenches and more rats than men ...

I tried to focus as my wings finally ripped from my body and were hurled somewhere beyond reality. I tumbled through time and space, too dazed to hope I might still be going in the right direction.

I could faintly smell white chocolate fudge. I thought of seaweed instead ... how the scent of a wave changed as it curled then crashed down ... the spray as white as the cheese on a fetta, spinach and pinenut pizza ...

And suddenly I was lying on a wooden pier, the blood from my back flowing cold onto the weathered planks.

Two cats watched me as they cleaned their paws. 'Miaow,' one greeted me.

I had no strength to move. Waves crashed and sucked on either side and under me. I could smell seaweed. And hot crusts, and anchovies too.

But that was impossible. Gaela had left the Leaning Tower of Pizza. There could be no scent of perfect pizza. They weren't even the same-coloured cats.

I managed to turn my head slightly. A shop stood at the end of the pier, and beyond it blue sea melted into the sky, like crushed tomato merged with melting cheese. The shop's sign just said 'Pizza'.

Something moved in front of me. I wondered if Titania had sent a dragon to swallow me as if I'd never been.

But then I saw two lengths of swirling fog, as black as midnight cats. The banshees. Were they going to chant my death song now?

'You need Band-Aid,' one of them said instead.

'More ... more than a Band-Aid,' I managed.

'We carry you to Gaela,' said the other banshee. 'She make you better.'

I tried to warn them that Titania might have more revenge to wreak. Nor could even a selkie heal the damage from my torn-off wings. But they lifted me in their furry, foggy arms, surprisingly warm for creatures of the night.

I had been cast from Fairyland forever. I had lost my wings. I might even lose my life. But the banshees were right. Gaela was all that I needed.

The world jolted around me as the banshees carried me along the pier. The waves crashed onto the sand. Sunrise was a small bright ripple on the horizon. Would I ever see another?

Far, far off, as if in a dream, I heard a fairy chant. Oberon's voice:

'Through the house give glimmering light,
By the dead and drowsy fire.

Every elf and fairy sprite
Hop as light as bird from briar.
And this ditty, after me,
Sing, and dance it trippingly.'

Now Titania sang the traditional fairy ending for Midsummer's Eve, as brightly and happily as if a fairy called Peaseblossom had never rudely interrupted her revels.

'First, rehearse your song by rote
To each word a warbling note.
Hand in hand, with fairy grace,
Will we sing, and bless this place.'

Oberon's baritone joined her for the last verse. I imagined all the fairies gathered there, about to carry out the final duties of Midsummer's Eve. But I would never join them again.

'Now, until the break of day,
Through this house each fairy stray.
To the best bride-bed will we,
Which by us shall blessed be;
And the issue there create
Ever shall be fortunate.
So shall all the couples three
Ever true in loving be.'

The King and Queen were commanding the children of Lysander and Hermia, Demetrius and Helena, Moth and Flossie to be happy. And what Their Majesties commanded must be done. I was the only fairy who had ever stood against them.

'*With this field-dew consecrate,*

Every fairy take his gait.

And each several chamber bless,

Through this palace with sweet peace;

And the owner of it blest

Ever shall in safety rest.'

Oberon's deep voice completed the chant:

'*Trip away; make no stay;*

Meet me all by break of day.'

The Midsummer's Eve revels were ended. It has all ended, I thought. But at least I was ending where I belonged ...

I heard a door open. The scent of pizza crust, of melted cheese and tomato sauce — a slightly different tomato sauce — greeted me. And the scent of seaweed.

'Pete!' whispered Gaela.

'He need bed,' said one of the banshees.

'No, I'll bleed all over it,' I murmured, trying to focus to see Gaela's face.

Then I felt her hands, her strong pizza-maker's fingers, somehow still with a hint of seal fur.

'In here,' she told the banshees.

And I felt sheets, a pillow. I wondered why, for surely selkies slept in the waves. But I could see nothing, only mist.

Then even the mist was gone.

CHAPTER 17

I woke alone. No, not alone. The delicious smells of baking pizza were all around me, and the song of the waves splashing in and pulling out below the wooden planks of the pier.

An orange and white cat rose from the end of the bed, stared at me expressionlessly, stretched, then jumped down and padded out the door.

Three seconds later Gaela appeared.

She looked … different. No more sack-like dress. No more hair pulled back in a businesslike ponytail. She wore blue silk trousers that billowed around her legs and were patterned with shells and fish, and her shirt was coral pink, the pattern almost too faint to see. Her glorious hair swung loose about her, as if still washed by ocean tides. One hand held a plate of pizza, the other a potion bottle. It looked familiar.

'Time for your next dose,' she said.

I looked at the flask suspiciously. 'Did an elderly fairy in a blue doublet with gravy stains bring that?'

She nodded. 'He brought a note too. It says to give you a sip of potion every hour and to rub a little on your back.'

'And I've been sipping it?'

She nodded. 'Even when you were asleep.'

What trick was Puck playing now? Was this enchantment to draw me back to Fairyland?

Then I realised the pain in my back was just a mutter, not a scream. I wriggled my fingers, then my toes, wrinkled my nose, then felt around to make sure other vital bits of me were still there. They were.

I was whole. And probably not quite human. But I was no longer a fairy either.

'Thank you, Great-Grandpa,' I muttered, and thought I heard a fairy chuckle. The old man had come through for me in the end.

I sat up cautiously, then leaned back on the pillows. They smelled of seaweed and sunlight with the faintest sweetest scent of perfect pizza dough.

Gaela sat on the bed next to me and watched as I sipped the potion, then bit into the pizza.

'Mushroom and three cheeses,' she said, then grinned. 'No anchovies.'

'Actually, I might get to like anchovies after we're married,' I said. 'You ... you will marry me, won't you?' I added anxiously.

Because of course I had never said ... and she had never told me ...

'Of course I'll marry you, idiot,' she said. 'I love you.'

'I love you too,' I said.

'Took you long enough to say it.'

'You should have tied me up with seaweed out in the ocean till I did.'

'Are we going to argue like this all our lives?' she asked, smiling.

'Probably. Are you going to keep trying to make me eat anchovies?'

'At least once a year, on our anniversary,' she promised.

We sat there grinning at each other for a while, till the room filled with the smoke of burning pizza and she dashed out to the oven. The cats were going to get lucky.

I'd eaten all the pizza and was lying down again by the time she came back.

'No great loss,' she said. 'Just a trial of apricot and cream cheese pizza. I'll experiment again when I have time to concentrate. But not today.'

'Not today,' I repeated, reaching up to kiss her.

My world had cracked apart today, but her smile could steady the universe. Yes, I thought vaguely, I really could get to love the taste of anchovies ...

After a while I asked, 'Where are we?'

'An island off Australia. They've never had a pizza shop here before. They make excellent local cheeses, and the sea serpent still brings me anchovies. The tomatoes they grow here are good too.'

'The sauce smells different.'

'Garlic,' said Gaela smugly. 'Lots and lots of garlic. The island grows that too. Purple garlic, white garlic, red garlic, fermented black garlic. They even have a garlic festival each year. There isn't a vampire around here for a thousand miles.'

Plus an island would have lots of beach, and maybe even a few shipwrecked sailors to rescue if she felt like a holiday. I should study CPR so I could help her.

'What's the new shop called?' I asked.

'I haven't been able to think of a name. Guyye suggested the last one.'

'How about Pizza Amore?'

'Perfect,' she said, and kissed me again.

The universe grew better still.

CHAPTER 18

Hippolyta died only ten years after her and Theseus's wedding, fighting side by side with her husband, defending Athens from another invasion. She loved Theseus till her last breath, and left him a son, Hippolytus. Theseus was driven mad with grief by her death. When his son died too, as a young man, Theseus threw himself off a rock, into the sea. Puck had been right. Theseus and Hippolyta had loved each other all their lives, though that love meant their lives were shorter than they might have been. Yet if I hadn't used the love potion on them, one of them would have died there on the plain of Athens, or even both. At least they had a few years of deep happiness together.

I expect Polchis knew love too. You'll find him in the history books: his father made him king of his own sub-nation. The books don't say if Polchis married, but a powerful werowance like him might have had several wives. I can't go back in time these days, so I have no way of telling for sure, but I suspect Polchis had a rich and fulfilled life, even if his people would soon face defeat and anguish. We have what we have, and must delight in every second of our joy while it lasts.

Nor do I know what happened to Demetrius and Helena. I'd like to think that Helena made Demetrius take the garbage out, do the washing, take the kids to the park each Sunday afternoon and rub her feet each evening. But they'd have had slaves to do all that, of course. I am sure Hermia and Lysander were happy. I hope they moved to live near Lysander's aunt, and Hermia never had to look at her father's sour face again. I bet she made Lysander honeyed baklava every Saturday, and even when they were ninety-four he still picked the first daphne flowers for her each year and told her she was more beautiful than their scent, and believed it.

A man called Shakespeare wrote a play about them all four or five thousand years later. One of our kids brought it home from school. It's not bad. I don't know how Shakespeare knew about Puck, but he features in it too. Puck gets around; maybe he and Shakespeare shared an ale or two at the Black Bear. Or maybe Puck led Shakespeare astray in the wood one night and whispered him a story in the dark.

Shakespeare even put me in his play, though I only had a few lines, and there was nothing about Gaela, the Fairy Floss, the banshees or pizza. But he mostly got it right.

We're still here, me and Gaela, at Pizza Amore. Gaela still enchants everyone who meets her. I'm used to it now.

Most of her old customers from the Leaning Tower of Pizza found us again. They come to the island for holidays each year, and enjoy the sand and surf and large amounts of pizza and ice cream.

The banshees make the ice cream, though they employ humans to serve the customers. There are no traditional banshee jobs any more. No one hears a banshee's song because everyone has the TV on, or they're distracted by their mobiles, and their windows are shut for the air-conditioning. 'Banshee Delight' is great ice cream, almost as good as my 'Passionfruit Supreme'. The table in the corner of Pizza Amore is permanently booked for four each Sunday night, because the banshees have two kids now. They're cute in a black fuzzy way, and they all love anchovies.

Our pizzas are still the best in the universe, and each one is rich with garlic. Gaela sautés the garlic cloves in olive oil till the harshness vanishes and there's only a subtle sweetness, but it's still enough to stop any vampire coming near Pizza Amore — or even getting too close to any of our customers for a long time afterwards.

It turns out that four hundred years of mixing potions is a great preparation for learning to cook. Apple pizza is still on the menu, but you should try my caramelised oranges with passionfruit ice cream (the secret ingredient is the orange blossom), or double chocolate cake with raspberry sauce. As for the hazelnut pavlova with cherries and choc fudge drizzle, Puck says it's the best dessert in ten millennia. He always has two helpings.

Puck visits every few years. It's good to see him, though I suspect he doesn't tell anyone in Fairyland where he's going. No point attracting attention. He trades gossip for pavlova and an artichoke and potato pizza, hold the cheese.

It feels right now, being Pete. We're even franchised.

No longer having wings means I can't circle the earth in forty milliseconds any more. I miss hovering on moonlight, but I'm still fast enough to deliver a pizza before the second note of 'Love Me Tender'. I'm still (sort of) immortal too, at least till the sun swallows our solar system.

Our eldest daughter, Bianca, was born with fairy wings, but we've cautioned her to keep them hidden till she's eighteen and has a better idea of what she wants from life. If she has a hankering for the Fairy Court, I'm sure Puck will take her under his wings, but just now she wants to be an astronaut.

The twins, Remi and Jade, are selkie, at least at night when we go swimming as a family, Gaela holding me by the hand, and the twins leading Bianca. They've rescued sixteen sailors already, plus a kid who fell off the rocks while fishing. The island's Emergency Services gave them medals for each rescue. We've pinned the medals up on the café wall, along with Bianca's school prizes for her portraits of her Great-Great-Grandpa Puck.

We chose our lives, Gaela and I, chose to be together, but it hasn't all been easy. Real life never is.

Gaela still hopes that maybe one day her parents, her brother or her sister, or some old selkie friend might call in to the island, even just to see our kids. But it hasn't happened yet.

The ripped flesh on my back may have healed, but the scars ache in cold weather. Sometimes I dream that I'm flying in and out of misty clouds, or hovering through time, and wake up smelling chocolate. Other times I wish I could drop in at Fairyland for a Dew Brew with Cobweb, or to see how Mustardseed is going; or I wonder what Moth is messing up, and how.

There are hassles when the flour isn't delivered, or the cheese goes mouldy; and days so cold the frost eats at your bones, or so sultry that you wish your too-solid flesh would melt. There's global warming, earthquakes, bushfires, traffic jams and wars: Gaela and I are part of it all now.

I could fix most of those problems just by squeezing some flower juice into the eyes of the politicians, so they decide to save a forest or a coral reef, or an island that's gradually vanishing under water, taking away its people's home. But I don't.

'Use it or lose it,' Puck used to tell me when I first learned to fly. He was talking about my wings, but it applies to freedom too. Most humans are free to choose how to live, and where and why, but how many of them really do?

If you don't fight for your freedoms, you may never have them; or notice that they're gone till it's too late.

But I don't go on about all this to our customers. They're here for pizza, not a lecture on free will.

And I'm just a pizza-maker now, with flour under his fingernails.

Great-Grandpa Puck says it best, really:

'If we shadows have offended,
Think but this, and all is mended,
That you have but slumbered here
While these visions did appear.
Give me your hands, and we'll be friends,
True love shall restore amends.'

AUTHOR'S NOTES

I never used to like Shakespeare's play *A Midsummer Night's Dream*. It made me uneasy. I only recently realised why. Only royalty has free will in that play. Hermia must die or become a nun; Demetrius believes he's entitled to a bride who doesn't want him; the human boy in Fairyland has no name; and no one wonders how Bottom feels after his night with a mysteriously enchanting woman. It is a play about those with power abusing it and using it for the most trivial ends.

But at last I realised that may indeed be exactly what Shakespeare intended. He wrote his plays under two absolute rulers: Queen Elizabeth I, who was wise as well as capricious; and James I, who was only sometimes wise, and also extremely superstitious and mostly mad.

Criticising either of them was a way to end up with your head on a pike.

In Elizabethan times, your religion was prescribed by the Crown, as were the colour and fabrics you were allowed to wear according to your rank in life. Even what you ate had rules: meat only on certain days, fish on others, no eggs or dairy during Lent, and many other rules. Or, rather, laws, for if you broke them you faced major fines, imprisonment or death.

Was *A Midsummer Night's Dream* the only way Shakespeare could criticise the capriciousness of his country's rulers; and a world in which a glover's son, like him, was supposed to become a glover, not a playwright or a gentleman? A world that made him suffer when he succeeded at last in going his own way?

This book, too, is about free will. Freedom can be given, or it can be taken. But once you have it, use it and defend it, or you may find it vanishes like a fairy overnight.

Gaela's Poem

The poem Gaela quotes is 'The Forsaken Merman' by Matthew Arnold. It was one of my three favourites as a child, along with Tennyson's poems 'The Lady of Shalott' and 'Break, Break, Break'.

I recited 'Break, Break, Break' in my first year at school to a slightly astonished teacher instead of a nursery rhyme. Never underestimate a child's love of words, or the song of poetry or story.

ACKNOWLEDGEMENTS

Unless an idea bites my neck at 2 am and won't let go — which does happen — this is the last book in the Shakespeare series that began with *I am Juliet*, then *Ophelia: Queen of Denmark* and *Third Witch*, with a detour to *The Diary of William Shakespeare, Gentleman*, where I offered reasonable evidence that Shakespeare faked his death.

I'm vaguely tempted by *The Tempest* from Caliban's point of view, but not enough to glue myself to my computer. Portia is tempting, but argues her own case far better than I could. I am intrigued by Antony and Cleopatra and Julius Caesar, but Shakespeare departs so far from history that if I write about their times, I'd rather do it free from the need to stick to Shakespeare's text.

My love affair with Shakespeare's work began with the sonnets as a child, then *Romeo and Juliet* in adolescence, and even survived the close textual study of *Hamlet* and *Henry V* in high school, mostly because of a brilliant English teacher, Mrs Gillian Pauli, who swept us into a love of the words rather than boredom. *Macbeth* captured me when I played Third Witch in a semi-professional production — the director and main players were paid. We witches were not, but I learned far more than lines from that production, including how heavy a broadsword is, and quite how much a play's meaning may be changed by an actor's or director's interpretation of a role.

Shakespeare wrote in hard times, when a hasty word might get your head chopped off. I suspect he not only wrote many versions of his plays, to suit the varied audiences, but also kept them loose enough so that they might be played in different ways.

Nor do I think he'd mind what I have done. Shakespeare took the work of others and made it brilliant. I've taken his work and made it twenty-first century. I hope he might at least say, 'A workable attempt, Mistress French.'

There are so many, many people to thank for the joy in writing this series: Cristina Cappelluto, who saw the potential in what would have seemed to others an odd proposal — putting what *might* be there into Shakespeare's plays; Nicola O'Shea for brilliant editing; Pam Dunne for the most expert proofreading possible, picking up inconsistencies we'd missed in the last fifty readings. (I like to think that missing details, like it was Tuesday in paragraph three and Sunday in paragraph four, or a character has three 'other' hands, means the story is so gripping that we miss them. We are all entitled to fool ourselves now and then.) Thanks, too, to the designers for the totally perfect cover for each book in the series, including Amy Daoud for the *Peaseblossom* cover.

But two people, as always, stand out: Angela Marshall, who takes a dyslexic's mess and turns it into a manuscript, as well as having a pack rat's knowledge of history like my own, except with (mostly) different hunks of knowledge in those packs. Nor does she rely on Wikipedia for her sources, but has gleaned them from letters, diaries et al. for over six decades, as I have. Because of Angela, I can write with confidence, because if I muck up entirely (as opposed to a position I can substantiate even if we cannot tell exactly what is true) Angela will let me know — with reference, details and suggestions.

And always, Lisa Berryman, whose friendship I value even more than her supreme editorship. The world works better if everyone simply accepts that what Lisa says is right. It also saves a writer much time too. Lisa does not let me get away with leaving out the hard bits with the mental excuse 'the reader can imagine that'. True, they can — but why should they have to put in the bits I find emotionally or creatively difficult if they are forking out time and/or money to read my book?

Mostly, though, I would like to thank you, whoever is reading this book. Somehow, miraculously, I have been given the career I dreamed of since I was three years old, as well as one that I can continue now I am partially disabled. (You might want to imagine me writing each book now with my left leg up on three pillows. On the other hand, better not.)

It has been a joy to write this series, but every book is written in partnership with the reader. As the Master said in *Henry V*, "tis your thoughts that now must deck our kings'. I hope we've both had happiness, adventure, intrigue, introspection, enlightenment, wonder, many giggles, some laughter, a few tears, as well as escape and friendship as we share these pages, even if we never meet.

Jackie French
Araluen Valley, 2019

Jackie French AM is an award-winning writer, wombat negotiator, the 2014–2015 Australian Children's Laureate and the 2015 Senior Australian of the Year. In 2016 Jackie became a Member of the Order of Australia for her contribution to children's literature and her advocacy for youth literacy. She is regarded as one of Australia's most popular children's authors and writes across all genres — from picture books, history, fantasy, ecology and sci-fi to her much loved historical fiction for a variety of age groups. 'Share a Story' was the primary philosophy behind Jackie's two-year term as Laureate.

jackiefrench.com
facebook.com/authorjackiefrench

The Secret Histories Series
1. Birrung the Secret Friend • 2. Barney and the Secret of the Whales
3. The Secret of the Black Bushranger
4. Barney and the Secret of the French Spies
5. The Secret of the Youngest Rebel

Outlands Trilogy
In the Blood • Blood Moon • Flesh and Blood

School for Heroes Series
Lessons for a Werewolf Warrior • Dance of the Deadly Dinosaurs

Wacky Families Series
1. My Dog the Dinosaur • 2. My Mum the Pirate
3. My Dad the Dragon • 4. My Uncle Gus the Garden Gnome
5. My Uncle Wal the Werewolf • 6. My Gran the Gorilla
7. My Auntie Chook the Vampire Chicken • 8. My Pa the Polar Bear

Phredde Series
1. A Phaery Named Phredde • 2. Phredde and a Frog Named Bruce
3. Phredde and the Zombie Librarian • 4. Phredde and the Temple of Gloom
5. Phredde and the Leopard-Skin Librarian
6. Phredde and the Purple Pyramid • 7. Phredde and the Vampire Footy Team
8. Phredde and the Ghostly Underpants

Picture Books
Diary of a Wombat (with Bruce Whatley)
Pete the Sheep (with Bruce Whatley)
Josephine Wants to Dance (with Bruce Whatley)
The Shaggy Gully Times (with Bruce Whatley)
Emily and the Big Bad Bunyip (with Bruce Whatley)
Baby Wombat's Week (with Bruce Whatley)
The Tomorrow Book (with Sue deGennaro)
Queen Victoria's Underpants (with Bruce Whatley)
Christmas Wombat (with Bruce Whatley)
A Day to Remember (with Mark Wilson)
Queen Victoria's Christmas (with Bruce Whatley)
Dinosaurs Love Cheese (with Nina Rycroft)
Wombat Goes to School (with Bruce Whatley)
The Hairy-Nosed Wombats Find a New Home (with Sue deGennaro)
Good Dog Hank (with Nina Rycroft)
The Beach They Called Gallipoli (with Bruce Whatley)
Wombat Wins (with Bruce Whatley)
Grandma Wombat (with Bruce Whatley)
Millie Loves Ants (with Sue deGennaro)
Koala Bare (with Matt Shanks)
Dippy's Big Day Out (with Bruce Whatley; concept by Ben Smith Whatley)
When the War is Over (with Anne Spudvilas)
Happy Birthday Wombat (with Bruce Whatley)

Discover the other books
in Jackie French's acclaimed
Shakespeare series ...

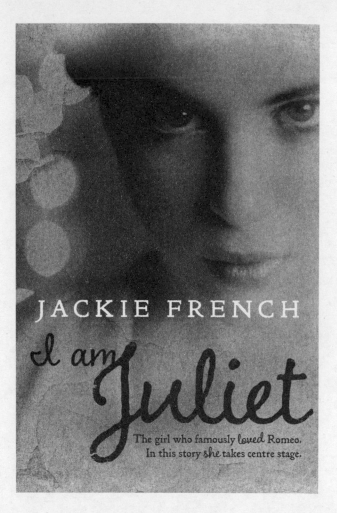

JACKIE FRENCH

I am Juliet

The girl who famously *loved* Romeo.
In this story *she* takes centre stage.

Everyone knows the story of Juliet Capulet and her love for
Romeo. The star-crossed lovers from the warring Capulet
and Montague families of Verona whose love was doomed.
But who was this girl Juliet?

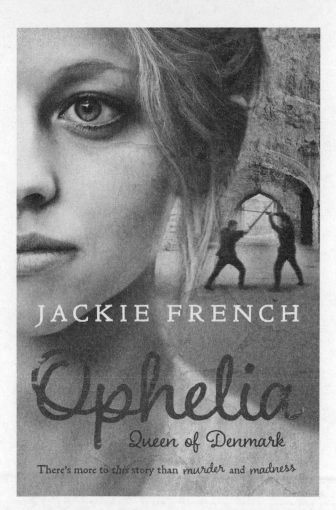

JACKIE FRENCH

Ophelia

Queen of Denmark

There's more to *this* story than *murder* and *madness*

She is the girl who will be queen: Ophelia, daughter of Denmark's lord chancellor and loved by Prince Hamlet. But while Hamlet's family stab, poison or haunt one another, Ophelia plans a sensible rule. Even if she has to pretend to be mad to make it happen ...

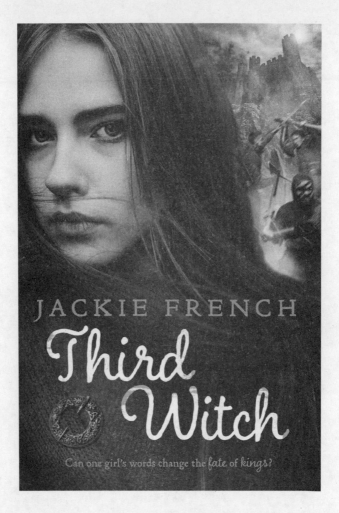

JACKIE FRENCH

Third Witch

Can one girl's words change the *fate* of *kings?*

Annie Grasseyes is not a witch, but when her mistress
Lady Macbeth calls for a potion to 'stiffen Macbeth's
sinews', Annie is caught up in plots that lead to murder,
kingship and betrayal.

How one man created the world's most enduring
love stories and mysteries ... and not just on the stage

JACKIE FRENCH

The
Diary of
William
Shakespeare,
Gentleman

He was a boy who escaped small-town life to be the world's most acclaimed playwright. A lover whose sonnets still sing 400 years later; a glover's apprentice who became a gentleman. But was William Shakespeare happy? And could he put down his pen forever like a true gentleman?